THE STORY COLLECTOR'S ALMANAC

# PACIFYING
## THE
# MIST

E.S. BARRISON

*E.S. Barrison*
*www.esbarrison-author.com*

Publisher's Note: This is a work of fiction. Names, characters, places, and incidents are a product of the author's imagination. Locales and public names are sometimes used for atmospheric purposes. Any resemblance to actual people, living or dead, or to businesses, companies, events, institutions, or locales is completely coincidental.

Content Warning: This book is rated 14+ due to child abandonment, suicide, and death.

Book Layout © 2017 BookDesignTemplates.com

*Pacifying the Mist/E.S. Barrison*. -- 1st ed.
ISBN 979-8-9929726-0-3

Dedicated to Grandma Rhoda & Grandpa David

Because you showed me not every victory needs to end with a bang.

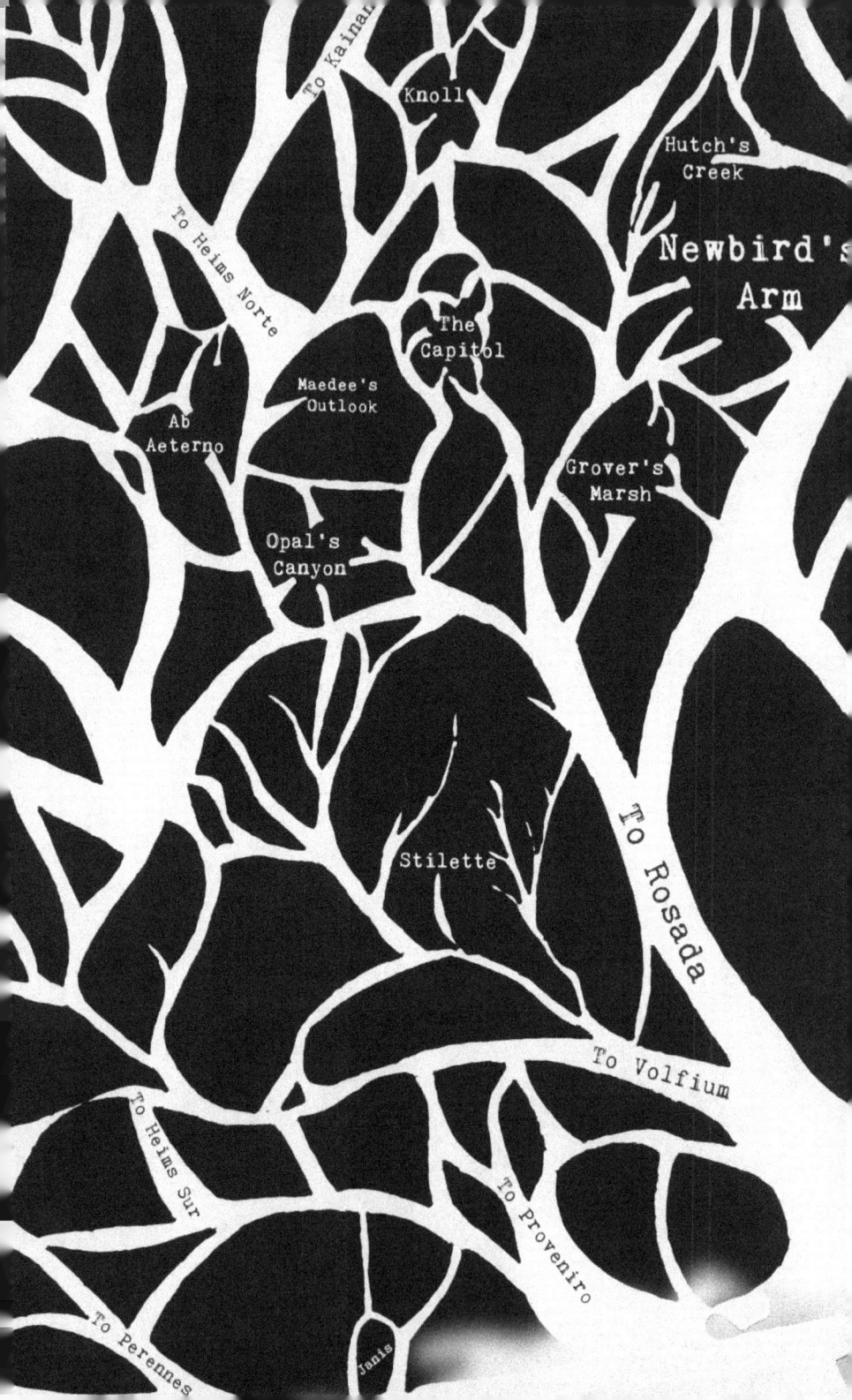

t

Graycott

To
Evylain

To Spinoza

To Delilah

Errat

To Yilk

See a more detailed map in the back of the book.

# The Council of Mist Keepers

### Ningursu
The God of Death

### Aelia
The Healer

### Tomas
The Peacemaker

### Julietta
The Painter

### Jiang
Null

### Malaika
The Cartographer

### Alojzy
The Architect

### Caroline
The Illusionist

### Brent
The Story Collector

# AL·MA·NAC

*a publication containing astronomical or meteorological infor-*
*mation, as future positions of celestial objects, star magnitudes,*
*and culmination dates of constellations.*

# FOREWARD

Not every story begins with sense.
Some begin with chaos, derived from madness and uncertainty. Others emerge from what seems like randomness.

But I'm not one to abandon even the strangest tales.

When I first learned of the Council of Mist Keepers, I thought I had gone mad. The mere idea of a coalition of beings destined to save the souls of the dead perplexed me. It seemed like a story plucked out of thin air and handed to me in an unedited jumble.

The Mist Keepers only provided so much guidance. Mostly, they kept their secrets close to their chest, hiding truths from even their own members. Through all of this, the overwhelming sensation of the Mist weighed on me, with few ways for me to return to myself.

That is until I spoke with Tomás.

I was unsure what to make of Tomás at first. Even after he helped me identify my constants, his actions ignited my suspicions. With the ability to read minds, Tomás uncovered my entire sense of self with a mere blink while wearing his own identity close to his chest.

But as I unraveled his past, it became clear that his experiences would serve as a blueprint for my future. This man, who always held himself with grace, followed a pattern similar to my own. Unable to keep his mind in order, he sought the constants in his life.

But not all constants remain consistent.

Well, except for Death itself.

While Tomás's story operates in the face of Death, it is also one of war and of peace. It is the story that victors often forget.

Because victors write about how blood wins wars, not individuals operating in the shadows.

But I do not champion bloodshed.

Because I'm the Story Collector.

- Brenton Rob Harley
Ninth Member of the Council of Mist Keepers
The Story Collector

# ONE

The voices had been speaking to Tomás since he was five years old.

Perhaps longer.

His first memory was of a single voice whispering "goodbye" into his head as a hooded figure left him outside of La Catedral in the heart of El Limra.

Tomás had lived there since, moving through La Catedral like a ghost while children came and went, joining new families and abandoning their old ones. The old matron, the Abedesa, never passed Tomás any regard, speaking of him as a sickly child with no skill, voice, or reason.

She was right. Tomás knew that. The voices, after all, spoke to him constantly. They reiterated each point, casting slurs on his intelligence and mocking his disheveled appearance. Some voices sounded like the Abedesa herself, while others reminded Tomás of the other children.

*He's a mute.*

*Dumb.*

*Can't even read.*

When Tomás had tried to read, the words blurred on the page, and the voices kept mocking his very attempt. Even when he spoke, different thoughts entered his head, infiltrating the most basic conversations.

So, he accepted that as his life: surrounded by voices and unable to fight them as they grew stronger.

They didn't stop, no matter what he did. At night, they floated into his dreams. During the day, they haunted him in the halls. And, whenever Tomás gathered in line with the others to receive his food, they screamed.

Like every time, the Abedesa eyed him, standing before two large bowls of gruel. She asked, "Maize or oat?"

Tomás stammered.

*Maize. I want maize.*

*Oat.*

*I couldn't care less.*

*Oat.*

*Maize.*

*They both sound disgusting.*

*Old hag.*

"Well?"

*Hurry!*

"Old hag!" Tomás shouted.

With that mere statement, the Abedesa slammed her spoon down, and for two days, she locked Tomás in his bunk without food. While the voices continued, at least in his room, they were more like whispers, allowing him to recite half-brewed prayers to the carvings of L'Corona Verde, the great Goddess of Life that watched over La Catedral and city.

Not that L'Corona Verde ever answered his prayers.

Without her guidance, perhaps it was best to keep quiet, stay to the corners, and mumble to himself and no one else.

For the next few years, as children left, adopted by families seeking the most remarkable and the brightest, Tomás stayed silent. Why would anyone adopt him? There were children in La Catedral who could read, write, count, and even perform magical feats. They could summon flowers and seeds, create sculptures from vines, and reignite the sleepiest trees. Of course, those children would find homes—and if not homes, a place amongst the King's Gardeniros in São Caméliosa to hone their skills in preparation for any oncoming battle.

So, when a tall man in a dark, tattered cloak walked in, seeking the brightest in the orphanage, Tomás did not even flinch. He remained in his corner, mumbling to himself, as the voices continued their relentless mocking.

*Oh, it might be me!*

*It won't be me.*

*I'll show him my garden!*

*He's creepy looking.*

"Shut up," Tomás hissed to himself, crossing his legs and bringing his head to his hands.

The Abedesa led the man through La Catedral, pointing out the different children. Occasionally, voices that sounded like the Abedesa herself entered Tomás's head.

*No, don't show him that one—they have not bathed in weeks.*

Tomás closed his eyes. Sleep did not help with the voices. They returned like beasts, clawing at his head, and he woke every morning with a migraine pounding against the sides of his head.

What he would give for silence...

But La Catedral echoed in a constant hymn.

"Those are all the children, senhor. Any of interest?" the Abedesa said, just within Tomás's hearing.

The man eyed the room, his bright silver eyes taking careful note of everything in his purview. "What of him?"

"Who?"

The man nodded toward Tomás.

"Tomás? He is not worth your time, senhor. In the ten years since his arrival, he has not shown intelligence greater than a mule."

"Well, mules are considered highly intelligent animals."

"It is but an expression. Tomás has no potential. He cannot read or write, talks to himself all the time. It is not worth your time, senhor. Someone like Brasia or Jorje certainly will fit your criteria."

"We can fix the inability to read or write," the man replied.

"Senhor!"

The man waved the Abedesa away. "I will come find you once I decide."

The Abedesa huffed and stormed back to her station overlooking the children.

*I know better than anyone what these children are like. Men! Pah!* a voice echoed.

The man watched as the Abedesa left before turning to Tomás. His silver eyes darkened as he approached, scanning Tomás up-and-down. Then he smiled, taking a seat beside Tomás.

Tomás looked away at once. He expected another voice to mock him, but this time, nothing entered his head. He furrowed his brow.

"Hello. Tomás, is it?" the man asked.

Tomás nodded.

"You have been here for ten years?"

Another nod.

"Why is that?"

Tomás stared at the man. He gulped.

"Go on. You can speak."

Tomás opened his mouth, speaking in a raspy, unpracticed tone, "Because I'm a loon."

"A loon?"

"Yes, senhor."

"Says who?"

"Everyone."

"And why is that?"

Tomás glanced over his shoulder. "Because everyone says so."

"But there must be a reason."

Tomás fidgeted. The voices didn't echo in his head, nor did they tell him what to say.

"You can tell me," the man said.

Tomás swallowed, then whispered, "I hear voices... all the time."

"Voices?"

"Yes...voices...that don't belong to me."

"I see..." The man's lip curled upwards. "Do you hear them now?"

Tomás paused. The voices still hadn't returned. "No."

"Did they stop when I arrived?"

"Um, yes senhor."

"Then you passed my test. You are exactly what I am looking for."

"Senhor?"

The man smiled. "You have a talent, Tomás, one that is limited to a select few. The voices you hear come because you are untrained, but I can train you to harness them and your untapped abilities. That I quelled your abilities proves to me you are the right choice."

"But what does that mean, senhor?"

"All in due time, Tomás." The man adjusted his cloak and said, "I will arrange your departure with the Abedesa. Say goodbye to your insignificant life here and any friends you have acquired. A long voyage is ahead of you."

"Senhor, wait! I am confused."

"Answers will come soon, Tomás. Do not worry. I will see you soon." The man smiled one last time at Tomás, then strolled away, back through the pews, towards the Abedesa's station.

Tomás stared after the man, unable to string together his own thoughts. It was one of the strangest interactions he had ever had.

Was it just the voices growing louder?

There was no way this man had any interest in him.

*He just spoke with the loon.*

*Why would he care about that mule?*

The voices returned in full force.

There was no way anything would change.

The man was just a figment.

A thought.

Nothing else.

# TWO

The Abedesa called Tomás into her office a day later. She handed him a piece of paper, with illegible squiggles across it.

"Congratulations, Tomás," the Abedesa said. "You have acquired yourself an apprenticeship under the senhor who visited yesterday. How? I have not a clue."

*He must have felt sorry for you,* the voice hissed in Tomás's ears.

Tomás stared at the paper, trying to read any of the words. But they jumbled on the page, dancing like the voices that kept him awake at night.

"He's arranged transport for you first thing in the morning. Prepare your belongings," the Abedesa said, then her face softened. "I honestly thought you would be here until you came of age…and then we'd send you onto the street. Glad someone saw something in you, Tomás."

"Thank you, Senhora," Tomás mumbled.

"I'll take you to the docks tomorrow morning for your transport. Rest tonight."

Tomás bowed his head once and left the Abedesa's office. The voices continued to follow him as he returned to his cot in the sleeping quarters shared with the other boys, quieting as he closed the door and found his cot. His quarters were empty, the other children out playing or conducting business around the cathedral.

Tomás struggled to wrap his head around what this man had seen in him. He had no skills. Since he had been in the cathedral, he spent most of his days in a trance-like state, just listening.

He reached for his bag under his cot. All his possessions sat in this bag. Nothing remarkable—a spare pair of trousers, an additional tunic, a pair of work boots. No letters. No old toys. Nothing.

He was just the resident loon, as the others said. The one who mumbled to himself, the one who talked to walls, the one who confused voices with his own thoughts. In the silence of the bedroom, Tomás at least knew his mind and thoughts were his own.

Tomás existed.

That he knew.

That he understood.

But who he was... Well, that was yet to be determined.

The next morning, the Abedesa walked Tomás to the docks. He rarely left the cathedral, only taking excursions once or twice a year. The city itself bustled, and the voices boomed as they walked through the streets.

*I need to go.*

*Where's the bread?*

*Mama? Mama, where are you?*

*Mierda!*

Tomás tugged at his fingers as he followed the Abedesa, trying to ignore the constant noise. It was like being in a crowded room or in the middle of a prayer service to L'Corona Verde. Constant echoes. Constant chants.

They grew quieter as they neared the docks. Upon emerging from the stone facade of the city and moving down through the valley of merchants and traders, the sea provided a quiet breath of peace. The voices still sang in a barrage of different languages, but they softened ever so slightly, so Tomás heard his own thoughts above their taunts.

The Abedesa led Tomás toward a dinghy ship, bobbing at the end of a dock. With its silver sails and old wooden planks, it didn't scream of authority or grandeur.

Tomás pulled at his fingers again, slowing his pace as they walked along the water. He'd never been this close to the sea; now, he'd be boarding a ship and letting it take him far away from this city. From home.

Even if he never quite felt a sense of belonging here.

An individual in a long regal coat and with wiry black hair greeted them. Their dark eyes narrowed, their lips curving into a frown. "So, this is the one they're sending my way this time, eh?"

"I assume you are Captain Huo," the Abedesa asked.

"The very one."

"Very good. Then this is Tomás." The Abedesa guided Tomás toward the captain and handed him the letter from the strange senhor.

The captain took the letter, sniffed it, then read through the words. They nodded once before turning toward a rather tall young crew member.

"Vardy!" They proceeded to call out something in a foreign tongue, before returning to Tomás and the Abedesa. "Varden here will get you situated. We'll leave in the evening, when the tide rolls in."

Tomás bowed his head, wincing as a barrage of foreign voices infiltrated his mind.

The Abedesa placed a hand on Tomás's shoulder. She didn't speak, but the mere sign of affection, despite her years of berating, quelled some of Tomás's nerves.

But not the voices.
Never the voices.

# THREE

Varden led Tomás to a small room below deck, equipped with a cot and a chamber pot. The man, no more than a couple of years older than Tomás, did not speak while nearly hitting his head against the pillars of the ship. Tall, with fair skin and dull red hair, his height was only one of the many fascinating things about him. What Tomás fought to shake was Varden's eyes: piercing red, as if someone jabbed a knife into them, filling the irises with blood.

When Varden finally did speak, his voice did not boom like a giant but melted across the air, like warm cheese on top of potatoes. "Dinner is at sundown, if you want to join. You can stay in your room, too. No one really cares—you are our guest."

"Thank you," Tomás mumbled.

"It is my pleasure." Varden laced his hands behind his back, and with a single nod of his head, he walked back through the narrow corridor and towards the deck.

Tomás sat on his cot. Through a small porthole, he watched as the waves bounced back-and-forth. Above, the crew mulled about, preparing for departure. With their activity, the voices whispered, a consistent buzzing in Tomás's ear.

In some ways, it provided solace; things never changed.

But that peace fell into the pit of his stomach. He was on a boat, yet he hadn't a clue where he was going...or why. That man from La Catedral could be sending him to the belly of a mythical dragon or into the arms of chanting sirens. Everything he said about being special, that had to be nothing more than smoke meant to distract Tomás.

The man wasn't even here!

Tomás pulled his legs to his stomach and pressed his head against the wall. He should have listened to the voices! They told him he wasn't special, that he didn't deserve to be saved. They had just been trying to protect him.

Right?

The boat lurched slightly. Tomás peered out of his porthole window. With the waves as its guide, the boat moved away from port.

Tomás swayed slightly, his head aching with each bobbing movement. The idea of food made his stomach tumble.

He hugged his knees tighter, unable to draw his attention from El Limra even as it became a mere speck on the horizon. This was it. There was no escaping what horrors lay on the waters.

And no escaping the voices that would follow him across the sea.

Seasickness marked the first week of Tomás's voyage. He could barely walk three steps without succumbing to nausea. Whether it was the rocking of the boat, the weaving voices babbling in foreign languages, or the fear of his murky future, Tomás couldn't be sure. He just kept to his room, accepting lukewarm food from Varden, and finding comfort in the stiff pillow on his cot.

After a week, Varden knocked on Tomás's door. Tomás fumbled it open a crack.

"I am not hungry," Tomás muttered.

"I only bring this disgusting leaf juice," Varden said, holding a cup of tea.

Tomás took the cup. "Tea?"

"Yes."

"Thank you..." Tomás returned to his cot and stared into the liquid.

Varden did not leave immediately, glancing around the small room. "The fresh air might do you well."

Tomás placed the cup on the table. "I can't."

"Why not?"

"I might vomit."

"You have hardly eaten. What will you vomit?"

"Whatever I have managed to keep down."

"Trust me, fresh air will do you well. Come, I'll help," Varden hoisted Tomás from the cot with one large arm.

*He is frailer than I thought,* a voice said.

Tomás froze, warmth radiating through his body at Varden's touch. But as soon as it arrived, he pushed Varden away, hopping back to the floor. "I can walk."

"Well, come. It is a lovely morning." Varden motioned for Tomás to follow.

Tomás brushed the sides of his tunic and followed Varden up toward the ship's deck. He shook his head, pushing aside the warmth still radiating in his cheeks. Instead, he kept walking, taking care with every step.

Each step rocked, swaying like the lanterns in the corridor. Even the ladder to the deck shifted beneath the rocking of the waves, tugging one way to the side as Tomás ascended.

Sunlight poured down as a blinding light on deck. Tomás squinted, letting his eyes adjust to the endless parade of blue across the horizon. Salt stained the air, and as he exhaled, the nausea disappeared.

But the voices returned with the crew, marching across the deck, securing knots, and tending to goods.

*Swear they're just having us do nonsense.*

*There aren't storms for miles. There won't be.*

*Wonder what's for dinner.*

Tomás cursed under his breath, and in a haze of voices, he wandered to the edge of the deck and peered out to sea. There was nothing but blue with an occasional touch of white from the clouds or the foam of the waves.

Nothing else.

"If I took a rowboat, I'd be free," Tomás mumbled to himself.

"Free?" Varden asked as he joined Tomás's side.

"Of the voices," Tomás replied.

"Oh. I see."

To Tomás's surprise, Varden did not inquire further about the voices.

Instead, he said, "Well, I imagine they'll help you with that."

"Who?"

"The Phrontistery."

Tomás raised his brow.

"The school. Where you are heading."

"I have not been told where I am heading."

"You haven't?"

"A man just told me that I was what he was looking for. He gave the Abedesa a letter, and she brought me here…" Tomás wrung his hands together. "The voices didn't tell me either."

"Did you not read your letter?"

Tomás flushed, looking away from Varden. "I cannot read."

Varden's head fell. "Oh."

Neither of them exchanged another word. Eventually, Varden disappeared to attend to his duties. Tomás stayed on deck, watching the waves for hours and basking in the silence until the sun set.

He didn't join the others in the dining hall, returning to his quarters without a word. Varden had been right; fresh air did help his sea sickness. But it didn't stop the barrage of questions and wondering, the constant dread of his future. Now, the question of a place called the Phrontistery sat at the forefront of his mind.

A school. What if he arrived, and upon learning he was illiterate, they turned him away?

How might he succeed without being able to complete such a basic task?

A knock on his door caused him to jump. Varden once again stood in the doorway, but this time, not with a bowl of cold gruel. Instead, he held a small stack of books and a few sheets of paper.

"I hope I'm not disturbing you," Varden said.

Tomás shook his head.

"Good. I..." Varden bit his lip, pondering his words. "I was wondering if I may help you learn to read. I am not very good at reading and writing in Vernnes since it isn't my native tongue, but...I can learn with you."

"People have tried to teach me before...but the voices have always interjected," Tomás said and flushed. "But I... appreciate the offer."

"Are the voices trying to stop you now?" Varden asked.

Tomás paused. The voices had returned to their whispers, distant enough that he could focus only on Varden. "No."

"Then why not try?" A twinkle shimmered in Varden's eye.

Tomás fidgeted and glanced at the ground. "Okay. We can try."

# FOUR

For the next fortnight, Tomás sat with Varden, trying to make sense of the jumbled letters on the page. Without the constant barrage of voices, he managed to focus on the words, reciting each sound aloud to himself. Varden read with him, patient as Tomás mouthed the "ahs" and "ohs" of the vowels and the rhythmic clicks and clacks of the consonants.

While two weeks did little to fill the void left behind by a lifetime of voices, as the final night arrived, Tomás strung together the simplest of sentences and wrote his name with an unsteady hand.

"If you keep practicing, I have no doubt you could read the most complicated texts," Varden said as Tomás closed the book.

"Perhaps," Tomás mumbled. To his surprise, the soft voices in his ear didn't mock him but whispered distant reassurances.

He locked eyes with Varden. There was a type of serenity with Varden, one that Tomás had never felt before. Friendship, companionship, it provided a warmth that he hadn't expected.

And there was something about Varden that left Tomás flustered. Every word came with thought, every movement gentle despite his giant limbs, and every smile sincere when it crossed his lips.

"You will do well at the Phrontistery, Tom. I do not doubt that," Varden said.

"Can you tell me anything more about this...Phron-tis-ter-y?" Tomás asked, sounding out each syllable of the word.

"No. Only that we have helped seven or so individuals travel there over the past three years. It's a school for those with special talents... but Captain Huo hasn't told me much else."

Tomás frowned.

"But you'll do well. I know it. You are eager to learn. Few others would sit here reading with a giant like me."

Tomás met Varden's eyes again, then turned to the ground. "You've been... kind. Quite kind. I have never had a friend like this before." He swallowed. "I... I shall miss you."

Varden took Tomás's hand in his and squeezed it. While his smallest finger stretched the length of Tomás's palm, he was gentle in his touch.

"I am most positive that we will meet again someday, Tom. But first, you must go harness your own abilities," Varden said.

Tomás squeezed Varden's fingers. The touch caused his stomach to twist, but he didn't want to let go of the one friend he'd acquired.

Varden continued, "Take the books. As a present from me. When I see you again, I hope that you'll read them back-to-front at least thrice. Then we can talk about them, share their stories, and debate their morals. Is that fair, Tomás?"

"As long as you promise we'll see each other again."

Varden released Tomás's hand, "That's a promise I'll keep."

*Because our paths are tied together.* A voice chimed in Tomás's head.

For once, Tomás hoped the voice was right.

They docked early the next morning, just as the sun rose, casting its orange glow over the town speckled in white. Icy chills reverberated through the air, sending shivers across Tomás's body, while crystalized flakes floated from the air.

"Ah, you may not have seen this before," Varden remarked, "It is called snow."

"Snow?" Tomás asked.

"It gets cold here, so water...freezes and falls from the sky."

"Oh..." Tomás glanced up at Varden. "I've never been someplace this cold before."

Varden removed his cloak and draped it over Tomás. "Stay warm, my friend."

Tomás smiled at Varden. The very action felt foreign to him, out of practice, like something pulled at the corners of his lips with thin threads.

Varden shared in the smile, and for a few minutes, they reveled in the comfortable silence, two friends letting the word "goodbye" hang in silence.

"Tomás!"

Captain Huo strolled toward him, a thick fur cloak covering their body. At their side, a thin sword glistened, clanking with the vials decorating their belt.

"We must go now," the captain motioned.

Tomás glanced back once more at Varden and dropped his smile.

"We'll meet again someday," Varden said.

"I hope so," Tomás replied.

"I know so."

Tomás grimaced, then after glancing one last time at Varden, memorizing his friend's orange hair and contemplative red eyes.

The captain led Tomás from the ship and down onto the snow-speckled docks. Tomás pulled up his cloak's hood as they stepped ashore. His feet wobbled, the unfamiliarity of land as mocking as the voices in his head. They still rambled in unfamiliar languages.

He gripped the edge of the cloak tight, focusing on the scratchy threads.

The captain led him to a young woman standing on the docks. She only looked a few years older than Tomás, with her pale skin highlighting the blotches on her face. She wore a thick wool coat. As she removed her hood, light brown hair bellowed behind her with the wind.

"Ah, Teodozia! I expected Lady Aelia to greet us," the captain said.

"The Lady is away on more pressing matters, I am afraid. She asked me to greet the newcomer in her stead," Teodozia responded. "Is this the one?"

"Ay, this here is Tomás of El Limra," the captain pushed Tomás toward Teodozia. "Go on, lad."

"Pleasure to meet you, Senhorita," Tomás bowed.

"Please, call me Teodozia," she returned the bow to Tomás. "And the pleasure is mine."

"Well," the captain interjected, "shame Lady Aelia is not here. Had some affairs to discuss with her."

Teodozia glanced at them, "I will deliver the news. Lady Aelia trusts me."

"Hmph, tell her that this is our last delivery. We have more pressing matters."

*Like war.* The voice hissed in Tomás's ear.

"Very well," Teodozia said and removed a small parcel from her cloak, "Nonetheless, this is for you."

The captain snatched the parcel, opened it, and smiled. "Very good."

"Glad it suits your liking," she said, then turned back to Tomás. "Come along. We'll get you situated. "

Tomás glanced back at the captain one last time and passed them toward the ship. Varden stood there, looking down at the dock. Their eyes locked for a moment.

He waved.

Tomás waved back, his smile itching with pain, before turning away with Teodozia.

# FIVE

Teodozia said little as they walked through town and out into a hilly pasture of white flowers pushing through the crystalized snow. The voices followed Tomás, once again in an unfamiliar language. He used the cloak to ground him, running his fingers through the material and pushing the voices into the back of his ears.

Only as the smoky shadow of a fortress emerged on the horizon did Teodozia finally speak.

"You had a long voyage here from El Limra, didn't you?"

Tomás nodded.

"I admire that you came with little information. We often give our new apprentices a better introduction."

"My choice was this... or be homeless when I turned sixteen," Tomás replied.

"I see," Teodozia slowed her walk. "What have you learned about us?"

"Just that some man came and spoke to me. He said that because the voices were quiet, I was the right one and that he had an opportunity for me."

"I see. So not much."

Tomás nodded.

*Of course, Lady Aelia gives me the hard job,* a voice said.

Before Tomás acknowledged the voice, Teodozia said, "Well, let me be the first to welcome you to the Phrontistery. Here, you and seventeen other disciples will train and learn to become Custocaligo...or, as I like to call us, Mist Keepers."

"Mist Keepers?" Tomás asked.

"They are the equivalent to Télifinifóros or Kifo Kabaya. I am not very familiar with the religion of your region, but I am sure you have one as well... a God of Death or something similar, responsible for releasing the souls of the dead."

Tomás wracked his brain. Despite growing up with the Abedesa's lessons, he had never been able to focus on the prayers or sermons. He only remembered L'Corona Verde, memorialized in vines and roots outside of La Catedral.

"I can't think of one," Tomás remarked.

"Really? That's remarkable. Most religions have woven the Mist Keepers into their stories.

"I was never one for stories or scriptures..." Tomás wasn't planning to tell Teodozia that he just learned how to read.

Teodozia waved it off. "Well, you are here now, and you are a Mist Keeper. The name seems to delight most disciples and even our teacher, Lady Aelia."

Tomás did not reply.

Teodozia continued, "I promise, you will learn much under Lady Aelia. She has been a Mist Keeper for a long time, and when she returns, she will teach you everything. But for now, let us get you situated. The others will be excited to meet you."

Teodozia took a step toward the fortress's shadow.

But Tomás hesitated.

"Are you coming?" Teodozia asked.

"I was wondering..." Tomás wrung his hands together. "Why was I selected?"

Teodozia thought for a moment, then replied with a smile, "The Mist chooses who it wants. Why? I haven't the faintest idea."

The fortress pulsated with smoke. Tomás's feet grew heavy with every step while his throat tightened. In some ways, it reminded him of the man who visited La Catedral, beckoning, powerful, and wise. He paused as they reached the unremarkable, wooden doorway. With no voices pooling at the front of his mind, Tomás weighed his choices. Should he run? Who would stop him if he returned to port, rejoined that ship, and stayed with his friend?

Teodozia placed a hand on his shoulder. "Come. They are waiting."

Tomás obliged, and with heavy feet, he let Teodozia guide him into the fortress.

Inside, a grand entrance hall greeted him. Around the long table, a cohort of other disciples sat pouring over a collection of books and yammering amongst themselves. Smoke, marred by different colors, moved like people.

As soon as the doors shut, everyone rose to greet him, speaking with excitement. The words molded together, and with each word, the voices returned with a vengeance. They climbed into Tomás's ears, tugged at his mind, and threatened to lock him into the same trance of his childhood.

He stumbled backward and crouched to the floor. His head spun. With the voices rising, the mere reality of his situation sank into his chest. They told him he was a *God of Death*! It sounded preposterous, even with the constant barrage of voices. He voyaged across the sea to a completely unfamiliar land to be taught by... *Death Gods*?

He pressed his head onto his knees and closed his eyes. Teodozia had been so calm when she told him, and until he entered the fortress itself and sat face-to-face with these other disciples, it hadn't quite solidified itself as reality. But now he was here, and so were the voices...

"I am a loon," he mumbled to himself.

Teodozia kneeled beside him and placed a hand on his back. "You have had a long voyage. Let us get you situated in a room, then you can rest. Yes?"

Tomás didn't reply.

"Cevin!" she called. "You have a spare cot in your room, yes?"

"Ay 'mam," a boy with rusty blond hair and a speckled nose replied. A crease sat on his upper lip as if someone had taken a knife and sliced it open.

"Will you take him? I'll start the lesson up here for the others."

"Ay." The boy approached Tomás and offered a hand. Tomás shook his head, clamoring to his feet and trying not to steal a glance at the boy's upper lip.

"A'ight, c'mon then—the rooms are this way," Cevin motioned for Tomás to follow him.

After glancing over one last time at Teodozia, Tomás followed Cevin to the other end of the hall, and down a small corridor. There, a narrow stairwell led them downstairs. Smoke seeped from the walls, and the building breathed with it. At least, once they reached the bottom of the stairs, the voices seemed to diminish, hissing instead of shouting, but always there.

"We got a room to share over 'ere," Cevin marched toward the third door on the left. It was no different than all the others, with thick wood and an iron doorknob. He opened it with a mere tap of his hand. "C'mon!"

Tomás paused, taking another gander down the hallway.

*What's wrong with him?*

*Is he okay?*

*He must be tired.*

Tomás shook back the hissing voice and followed Cevin inside the room.

An unremarkable room with two narrow cots greeted him. On the left side, papers lay strewn on the floor, with a pen and well of ink sitting perched on the nightstand. Ink stained the table's surface.

"So yeah, that side is mine. Sorry about the mess— been alone in here for a few months. I'll hand those letters off to one of the ghosts soon, and they'll send them where needed. But I made sure they didn't end up on your side, a'ight? That right side... It's all yours!"

Tomás walked into the room and placed his bag on the narrow cot. "Thank you."

"The pleasure is mine." Cevin grinned again, the crease on his lip tugging the smile further upwards than normal.

Tomás turned away, attention locked on his bag. "Is it okay if I am alone for a while? I need to rest."

"But of course. I'll come fetch you for mealtime."

"Thank you."

"But of course," Cevin said, then exited the room, closing the door gently behind him. Alone at last, Tomás collapsed on the bed, closing his eyes to push the voices away.

Not that they ever listened.

# SIX

Despite Tomás's demurrals, the next morning, Cevin dragged him back upstairs, where the disciples gathered in a small sitting room around Teodozia. As they hurried down the corridor, that colorful, human-like smoke whisked past them. Tomás froze as one gasp of smoke moved through his body, nothing more than the wind.

"Ignore the ghosts. They have their own agenda," Cevin said as he opened the door to the sitting room.

Tomás didn't question Cevin and entered the room.

The disciples sat in a half circle in the room, watching as Teodozia wrote on the slate wall in Vernnes. Tomás understood a few of the words. He mumbled the alphabet to himself, sounding out each word.

"To-day's Les-son... The stor-ee of...of..." He frowned, then turned to Cevin. "What's that word?"

"Ningursu. Our leader."

"Ningursu?"

Before Cevin responded, Teodozia called, "Cevin, Tomás, please take a seat. We'll be having our lessons in Vernnes until Tomás acquires other dialects."

Tomás raised a brow, taking a seat beside Cevin. What did she mean by 'acquire other dialects'?

But apparently, that would be a lesson for another day.

"Very good." Teodozia smiled, then turned back to the slate wall, scribbling a few more words as she spoke. "To-day, we're going to review Ningursu's story—which I believe is paramount to understanding who we are."

A few disciples groaned.

"Yes, I know. Many of you are already aware of Ningursu's story, but we have some newcomers, and it is important that we all understand his tale. It is only then that we can come to terms with our future."

The murmurs subsided.

Teodozia continued, "Ningursu, as any god, is time-less. He discovered the power of the Effluvium—or Mist, in simpler terms—thousands upon thousands of years ago. He was the first to harness its power... and help souls, at last, cross into their peaceful resting place.

Whether that be the Effluvium itself or as souls wandering this earth. He saved humanity."

Teodozia spoke in a sermon-like dictation that reminded Tomás of the Abedesa. And, just like all of the Abedesa's lessons, the voices proved to speak louder. They overlapped with each other, oscillating between a variety of languages. Some slipped into Vernnes, echoing in Tomás's ear.

*I'll believe this when Ningursu actually shows up.*

*Thousands of years old? Doubtful.*

*He must be so powerful!*

Tomás lowered his head and closed his eyes.

Cevin nudged him. "Ay, listen—this is good stuff."

Tomás inhaled, then peered back at Teodozia.

Teodozia seemed to go into a trance while telling the tale, perfectly rehearsed. "Yet, despite his strength, Ningursu has his fair share of enemies. He has angered powerful rulers, many of whom he has defeated to protect the balance between Life and Death.

"But I think it is important that you learn everything you can about Ningursu...for now, we face a new foe. This foe was once Ningursu's dear friend...Tehuti Kek, the ruler of Merton. Ningursu and Tehuti Kek have had a friendship for centuries, one that they believed would be of mutual strength. But, over the years, the two have grown apart. While Ningursu has focused on maintaining the balance of Life and Death, Tehuti Kek has dabbled in dark magic that threatens this very balance.

"For a long time, Ningursu believed he might quell his friend's desire. But Tehuti Kek soon learned the true strength of this magic. With it, they created an army of magically inclined immortals, which threatens everything we, as Mist Keepers, believe.

"Ningursu confronted Tehuti Kek, of course, but they have not retreated from their magical endeavors. So now, Ningursu has vowed to defeat these immortals, gathering allies from the Effluvia region and beyond. But even with these allies, he cannot act alone. Therefore, he sought more Mist Keepers—like all of you—to end Tehuti Kek's reign once and for all."

No one spoke. Even the voices fell silent with the statement. Even if everyone had known this, the mere statement exasperated the situation. They were selected for a reason.

Yet, Tomás fidgeted at the thought. How was he supposed to help defeat an army? It seemed rather doubtful. Besides, how could he be a Mist Keeper if the voices continued their taunting?

Tomás struggled to pay attention to the rest of the lesson. Teodozia detailed Ningursu's life, from his childhood to his discovery of the Mist, in a practiced sermon. But with the voices mocking in exasperation, he did not commit the story to memory.

Once Teodozia concluded the lesson, rather than heading to the galley with the others for food, Tomás was quick to retire to his room. There, he sat on the bed, running his hands over the cloak from Varden. Already, the sound of Varden's voice had become a worn memory.

"I should've stayed on the boat," Tomás said aloud as he stroked the cloak. He did not fit the ideal picture of a Mist Keeper. How could someone like him protect everything Ningursu built? He couldn't fight. If he entered a battlefield, how loud would the voices be? Would he even be able to think?

They never left.

Whispering...

Repeating...

Garbled in unfamiliar languages.

He brought his knees to his chest and closed his eyes as their onslaught grew. "Go away, please..."

"Well, it's my room too, y'know." This time, the voice was real.

Tomás looked up, where Cevin stood in the doorway carrying a bowl of potatoes and a cup of tea.

"I just need to be alone...my head hurts." Tomás closed his eyes again.

"Ye, it's a lot to take in, isn't it?" Cevin placed the meal on the end table and sat on his cot across from Tomás.

The voices echoed again in Tomás's head, an unfamiliar language, seeming to almost laugh.

"No...it's not that. It is...well...there is no way that I can be a Mist Keeper," Tomás replied, "I'm a loon."

"Nah, you're definitely one of us."

"No. I have nothing special about me.

"Trust me, Ningursu and Aelia never make a mistake."

"Well, they did with me," Tomás huffed. "Why would they want someone who hears voices all the time!?"

"Voices?" Cevin frowned.

"All the time, my whole life. They are always talking—so how would I be able to help Ningursu if they never stop!?"

"Well...what are they saying now?"

"I don't speak the language they're speaking."

"Hm." Cevin leaned forward, furrowing his brow, his gray eyes weighed with thought. "Y'know, back when I first discovered my magic, I thought I was going a little mad, too."

"Your magic?"

"Ay, my magic. Y'see, all the Mist Keepers have magical talents. The Effluvium grants us this magic, and Ningursu and Aelia find other Mist Keepers because of it. Each disciple has unique abilities. Orvil can recreate static images of buildings and plants, Elva can find any object she puts her mind to, and Teodozia can recant anyone or anything's story with a mere touch. Everyone is different."

"But I don't have magic."

"Don't be so certain. I never thought I had magic. Growing up, I used to be jealous of my sister. She has magic. But one day, I realized I have it, too. It was strange...confusing. But eventually, I accepted it."

Tomás shook his head. "But I—"

Cevin held up his hand. "Let me finish. You may find we are more alike than you realize."

Tomás's shoulders sank, keeping his gaze fixated on Cevin as he continued.

"See, my magic allows me to integrate with the senses of others. So, I can see what people see, hear what they hear, taste what they taste, smell what they smell, and touch what they touch. I didn't notice it at first, but suddenly, I sensed things that weren't there. I couldn't describe it...and it was disorienting at first.

"But one day, my sister, Edith, stole a piece of sugar cake from the bakery. My mouth started to taste like sugar, so I went to the bakery... and there she was, eating it! So, we did some tests and discovered that I somehow was sensing everything she did. We thought it was 'cause we are siblings and all, but it seemed to randomly switch, as the next day I smelled apple blossoms, and we weren't anywhere near an orchard." Cevin paused, meeting Tomás's eyes. He grinned. "We kept experimenting. If I didn't have Edith, I might have lost my head uncovering the truth. But...instead, I learned all about myself. So, what I'm saying is...perhaps you need a friend to help you uncover your magic. Because I don't think those voices are just in your head."

Tomás raised his eyebrow. "What do you mean?"

"Here, let me try something...in a few seconds, tell me what the voice says." Cevin leaned back, his smile wide. His scarred lip curved slightly too far to the right, punctuating his cheek with a dimple.

Tomás turned his attention to the floor and gripped his hands together. He didn't like the idea of opening his mind to the voices.

"Go on," Cevin said.

Tomás obliged.

When the voice came, it sounded like Cevin.

*Hi there, Tomás. If you hear this, reply with the word 'green.'*

Tomás glanced back at Cevin, "Green?"

"Like your eyes," Cevin replied, that smile growing even wider. "You can hear thoughts, Tomás! You've got Mist of the Soul—like me!"

Before Tomás replied, Cevin spoke in his head again.

*See! Now you can hear me right here!*

Tomás gawked at Cevin. A ripple shook through his body as they locked eyes.

"I can hear thoughts," Tomás whispered. "I'm not... imagining things."

"I told ya! You're just as special as everyone here, Tom. You're a Mist Keeper!"

# SEVEN

Knowing that the voices were thoughts, Tomás hoped his life might get easier.

Yet each day, as Teodozia carried on with lessons, his head only continued to ring. He lost focus as she reviewed the different religious histories from across the globe. As fascinating as it may have been to learn about the interconnection between religion and Mist Keepers, Tomás instead spent those hours focusing on the voices. Who did they belong to? What could he learn from them? What secrets did they hold?

And was it right for him to even intrude?

After lessons each day, he retired to his room, where he gripped Varden's cloak and flipped through his small collection of books, recanting the reading lessons he had shared with Varden. What would Varden have thought of his magic?

Would the voyage have been easier if Tomás had understood his powers then?

He reflected in silence, accepting meals from Cevin in the evening and sharing in reticence.

Over the weeks that followed, despite his fleeting attention, Tomás observed the other disciples. As Cevin said, they each held a unique type of magic, ones that solidified how they'd serve Ningursu. A girl named Imelda could alter landscapes to temporarily emit a different sort of façade in what Teodozia called the Mist of the Surrounding. Meanwhile, a fellow called Loukios could ignite anger and fury inside everyone in the room, altering their emotions in what they called the Mist of the Soul. Then there was Estefano, who could recreate images as he played the flute in an act known as the Mist of Distortion. Teodozia elaborated on each of these types of Mist, different ways in which their powers might come together and be rectified, while each of the disciples performed.

But none behaved like Tomás's magic, locking him in a haze, altering time and reality like a dream. Where did he belong? What if he wasn't any type of Mist at all?

Yet, Cevin never let Tomás slip too far.

"Ay, Tom," Cevin entered their room one day after class.

Tomás did not look up from his book, reciting the same lines to himself over and over again. *Some believe that peonies hold power. But the Gardeniros put their faith in the camellia.* The book was about the history of São Camélosa, the capital city of his home country of Gonvernnes. Varden had placed it in the pile of books he had given Tomás. Already, Tomás had read it three times, absorbing the history of his home while reveling in momentary silence without foreign thoughts.

Cevin tapped the top of Tomás's book, "Ay, you hear me?"

"Yes, I apologize," Tomás sighed and lowered the book.

"Good," Cevin plopped on the bed across from Tomás. "Listen, I get those voices of yours are cumbersome. So, I, well, I translated my notes into Vernnes for you. Took a lot of 'em back when I first came here... and I can tell you like reading 'cause the thoughts aren't there to bother you. So, ye, here," Cevin held out a pile of parchment paper. "Hope you can read my handwriting. It's not very elegant."

Tomás took the paper and stared at the writing. His throat tightened. "You didn't have to do this."

"Yeah, well...I wanted to."

"Why?"

"You know to...um...succeed. Ye, I want you to succeed." Cevin's turned his attention to the end table.

"I appreciate it...but, as long as the voices are rambling...I doubt that will be possible."

"Well, have you tried to think of your constant?"

"My what?"

"Your constant." Cevin's smile returned. "Don't you have a constant?"

"I...I do not know."

"See, back in Eis, where I grew up, the most important thing in life is our constant. We usually reserve it for love, but it can be anything that makes you feel at home. Back when I noticed my magic more, I chose my sister as my constant. She was there for me through thick and thin. Do ya've something like that?"

Tomás frowned. "Not really. I was orphaned at a young age. I don't remember my family."

"Well, there has to be something that feels like home for you."

Tomás gripped his cloak in one hand and shook his head.

"Well, think about it. And once you find it, when the voices get too loud, use it to ground you, a'ight? Because even if the voices scream, your constant is still there."

Tomás bowed his head, still keeping his fingers laced into the cloak. On his lap, Cevin's notes seemed to beckon him with similar kindness.

Kindness... Could that be a constant? Two young men had offered a piece of themselves to Tomás, to help him succeed. Yet, they hadn't been constantly there in his life...so how could they be a constant?

But their kindness was unwavering.

Constantly there.

Pacifying Tomás.

And bringing him peace.

# EIGHT

T omás cut a strip from the tattered edge of the cloak and wove it into a bracelet. As winter turned to spring, it became far too hot to wear the cloak, but when the voices grew too loud again and he failed to differentiate one from another, the small strip helped him return to his constant. He also kept Cevin's notes in his pocket to review, learning everything about Ningursu and Aelia and the Mist Keepers. According to Cevin's notes, Ningursu had been alone for centuries. He attempted to introduce new Mist Keepers to the Effluvium, but each one failed, so continued to wander the earth alone. While he did communicate with the living, pushing aside the Mist and working with seers to connect with them, it was a lonely existence. Even the immortals did not understand his burden.

Finally, he met Aelia. She used her magic to heal both the living and the dead. How? Even Cevin didn't quite understand. While Aelia was their teacher, in theory, she wore her magic close to her chest, only revealing her abilities to those who needed to know.

In some ways, Aelia was more of an enigma than Ningursu...at least based on Cevin's notes. So, when Teodozia told them that Aelia would be returning, nausea captured Tomás, and as soon as class ended, he rushed back to his room. With his cloak as a blanket, he pulled his constant reminders of friendship and kindness close; Varden and Cevin told him it would be okay. So, he had reminded himself.

Constantly.

Despite the summertime heat, the next day, he wore his cloak to class. Teodozia did not join them, leaving all the other disciples babbling with excitement. The voices intermingled with their babbles. Tomás still understood little of the other languages, except for Aelia's name passed around like a serving platter and haunting every set of lips.

"I think Teodozia is meeting with Aelia now," Cevin whispered to Tomás. "I caught a glimpse of her sight."

Tomás nodded, playing with the edge of his cloak. Around him, the commotion continued.

Everything froze as the doors opened to the class-room. Teodozia walked in first, taking her place against the wall, her dark cloak transforming her into a shadow. A beat passed.

Then, Aelia entered. A tall, thin woman with dark eyes, she flowed into the room like a river. Her dark blue dress cascaded behind her, while tendrils of Mist floated around her as if she walked on a cloud.

*She always looks this regal.* Cevin's voice echoed in Tomás's head.

Tomás glanced at his friend. Cevin smirked.

Aelia took her place at the front of the classroom. She scanned the room like a hawk, her lips drawn in a wide frown. On her head, piles of dark brown hair sat, almost like a bird's nest.

"Eighteen?" she asked Teodozia.

"Yes, my lady," Teodozia replied.

"Shame we could not find more... but this will have to do," she turned back to the class. "I require each one of you to meet with me today. We must assess your progress at once."

*She has never been one for niceties.* Cevin whispered in Tomás's head.

Tomás nodded.

"I wish to meet with the newest cohort first," Aelia continued, "Teodozia, send them my way, will you?"

Before Teodozia replied, Aelia marched from the room, the Mist vanishing with her as she shut the door.

Teodozia led Tomás and the two other newcomers, the twins called Ívar and Elva, to Aelia's private suite. While Ívar and Elva chatted with excitement, Tomás trailed to the back, clutching tight to his cloak. Ívar and Elva were lucky—they had each other as they faced Aelia. He wished Cevin had come with him, but that wasn't aloud. So now, he had to face Aelia...alone.

Ívar and Elva met with Aelia first, leaving Tomás alone in the hallway with Teodozia. He fidgeted, attention fixated on the purple tapestry on the far wall.

"Do not be scared, Tomás. Aelia is only here to help," Teodozia said.

Tomás frowned.

"Do not fret. You have been doing better. I can tell," she continued.

"I do not feel as though I am doing better..." Tomás mumbled.

"Progress often hides from its beholder... but outsiders see it without qualms."

Tomás picked at a loose string on his cloak.

"I understand if it is hard to believe now, but trust me. You have already succeeded."

They returned to a shared silence until Ívar and Elva returned. The excitement they shared had vanished, leaving behind a much more sorrowful expression. Their thoughts echoed in an unfamiliar tongue, filled with the same sort of defeat.

Tomás's entire body froze. What had Aelia said to them? What stole their exuberance?

Teodozia didn't let Tomás ponder for long. "Go on in, Tomás. She is waiting."

Tomás's knees shook as he entered the room. Golden drapes hung on the wall, creating a glow around Aelia as she sat at the head of the table. In front of her, a porcelain bowl sat containing a mysterious silver liquid.

"Sit," she ordered, motioning to the seat beside her.

Tomás obliged.

Without a word, she took Tomás's hand, examining its creases. Her chilled fingers danced across each groove while the Mist wove its way between Tomás's fingers.

Then, she lifted Tomás's hand into the basin. The strange liquid bubbled around his hand, then settled. For a moment, Tomás swore he saw shadows on its surface.

"You have potential," Aelia said, "but your fortitude is concerning. We shall review in the coming weeks."

Tomás stared at her. Her thoughts did not infiltrate him, masked just like the man who had found him in La Catedral.

Aelia dropped his hand. "You are dismissed."

Tomás slowly rose from the table, bowed, and left the room. Weight had lifted from his shoulders, a single word echoing around his head: *potential*.

# NINE

Cevin babbled about his meeting with Aelia to Tomás all evening. Unlike Ívar and Elva, Aelia's feedback had been excellent, complimenting Cevin's ongoing growth and success as a Mist Keeper.

"And what did she tell you, huh?" Cevin finally asked as he sifted through a few papers on his end table.

"She said I had potential," Tomás replied as he picked at the edge of his cloak.

"That is high praise from Aelia! When I first met her, she told me it'd be impressive if I lasted a year. Look at me now! I can't wait to write Edith to tell her all about it. She's been worried about all of this, but I kept telling her that my training was going well. But she's always nervous about me."

Tomás smiled. Cevin's confidence was unmatched. What Tomás would give for a share of that emotion. It truly transformed Cevin into one of the most beautiful people Tomás had ever met. His gray eyes dazzled whenever he spoke, and despite his misshapen smile, there was something about it that left Tomás's heart aflutter. Yet Tomás did not dwell on these sentiments, falling instead into anxiety as the morning approached.

That next morning, Teodozia woke them before the sun rose, beckoning everyone to follow her from the fortress and into town. Tomás trailed toward the back with Cevin, fiddling with his handmade bracelet.

*I think they are having us practice releasing souls.* Cevin whispered in his head.

Tomás nodded. While Teodozia had told him the duty of the Mist Keepers was to guide souls into the next phase of existence, he had yet to conduct such a task. Or, really, to see one performed at all.

So Teodozia led them down the road, walking for over an hour, to a small village. Rather than entering the paved streets, they stayed at the edge of the village, where the field of white flowers beckoned to them like snow. There, amongst the foliage, misshapen rocks inscribed with text peeked out of the flowers.

Aelia stood in the center of the field, a silver dress cascading over her body, blending seamlessly into the surrounding fog.

"Ívar, Elva, Tomás - come join me. I shall show you how to conduct a release," Aelia beckoned. "Teodozia, have the others conduct at least three releases. The more, the better, but three is the minimum."

"Yes, my lady," Teodozia motioned for the others to follow her.

Tomás exchanged a quick glance with Cevin.

*It will go a'ight, I promise.* Cevin echoed.

Tomás swallowed, twisted his bracelet, and then followed Ívar and Elva over to Aelia.

Aelia spoke, punctuated and to the point, "The release is a quintessential part of being a Mist Keeper. At our core, it is our job to release the souls of the dead. Otherwise, they will be stuck in the land of nightmares, Nocturna, for all eternity. If you cannot conduct a release, your magic will never meet its full potential. With each release, your potential and magic will grow." She eyed each of them carefully. "Now, to release a soul, first we must find one. Right now, we are in the old burial grounds for the Schani people. While we have released many of the souls here, there are still hundreds we have yet to uncover. Since this is your first release, I have already located where a handful of souls are waiting. Come now, I will show you."

Aelia left no room for questions, heading at once down the hill and through the field of white flowers.

Tomás followed, running his fingers over their petals. As he touched one of them, the petals rescinded, causing the flower to wilt.

He frowned before refocusing on Aelia. Whispers filled his ears, unfamiliar and repeating in circles as if trying to call out for him. He twisted the cuff again, trying to focus on his constant.

But the voices did not weaken.

Aelia stopped at the bottom of the hill and turned back to them. "There are three souls waiting for their release within this vicinity. Who would like to go first?"

Ívar and Elva raised their hands in unison.

"Ívar, you will start."

"Can't Elva and I work together?" Ívar asked.

"As I told you yesterday, codependency will lead to your failure. Mist Keepers have always operated alone."

"But—"

"That is how it must be."

Ívar pouted.

"Now, if you are so inclined, I need you to focus on your magic. It will guide you to the soul."

"How?" Ívar asked.

"Well, with your abilities, you can manipulate color, yes? Then tell me, what color do you see when you close your eyes?"

Ívar closed his eyes. "A grayish blue... I think. It keeps flickering."

"Then keep walking until the color stabilizes. That is where the soul will wait for you. Once there, wait for my next instructions." Aelia turned to Elva. "Now you do the same, but with *your* magic. What do you see?"

Elva also closed her eyes, "A...circular object. I think it is a rock. Or...no. A seashell."

"Keep walking until it stabilizes, then wait for my instructions." Aelia returned to Tomás.

He squirmed.

"Now, Tomás...you need to listen rather than see. Listen to the voices and follow them until the words are clear."

"Yes, senhora. But what if I cannot understand what the voices are saying?"

"You will soon. Remember, there is an exchange for the release. The souls will pay for your services in knowledge...such as knowledge of language."

"I...am not sure I understand."

"You shall see. Now go."

Tomás nodded and twisted his bracelet. After a deep breath, he let the voices fill his head. While the rambles of Ívar and Elva echoed, he found an unfamiliar voice repeating a muffled word.

He walked toward it, letting it solidify. Soon, the words formed, bearing a familiarity to his own tongue.

*Halme...*

*Helme...*

*Hel me...*

*Help me!*

He froze, staring at the spot on the ground. It was nothing remarkable, covered with the same white flowers as the rest of the field.

Aelia called out from her spot in the distance. "Now, I want you to place your hands on the ground and focus on whatever you see or hear. Imagine reaching out to that object or voice, and pull it towards you."

Tomás obeyed despite the obscure request. He dug his fingers into the ground.

*Help me!*

"I'm here," he said to the ground.

*Help me!*

He pressed his head to the ground, whispering to it, "I'm here—let me help."

*Help me!*

*I'm here! Let me help!* his thought echoed back.

With that mere thought, he fell forward and didn't stop falling.

*The voice rang.*

Help me!

*It kept echoing through darkness.*

*Begging.*

*Tomás saw nothing.*

*Blind.*

Help me!

*He reached his hand out into the shadows.*

HELP ME!

"I'm here!" *He grabbed at the dark.*

*To his surprise, it grabbed back.*

"I'm here to help," *he said again, pulling the darkness close to him.*

*Cradling it.*

*Quelling it.*

*And promising it all would be okay.*

Tomás stopped falling, face-planted in the dirt. He raised his eyes, where the smoke circled around him.

It continued to echo the words of the soul.

*Help me!*

"I did..." he gasped.

New voices began their onslaught, spinning around him, clawing at his head.

*Help me!*

*I'm dying.*

*No!*

*Stop!*

*I never said I love you.*

*Help me!*

Tomás held his head, the voices growing more pronounced and defined.

Just like the smoke.

And like the pounding in his ears.

Clawing...

Grappling...

Stabbing...

Until he fell into darkness again.

# TEN

"Tom? Tom!"

Cevin's real voice pulled Tomás awake. He opened his eyes at once, blinking away tears as his vision solidified.

He lay on a cot in an empty stone room. Ívar and Elva slept in the cots to his left. The colorful shadows of ghosts mulled about their beds, tending to their sheets. On his right, Cevin sat beside him, panic in his pale eyes.

"What happened?" Tomás asked, sitting up slightly. His head pounded, but only whispers haunted him.

"You conducted your first release, but you passed out. That's normal and a'ight, but I was worried...you've been asleep for a couple days. I was finally able to sneak away to visit you. Aelia has kept this area off limits." He helped Tomás sit up, pushing a cup of tea into his hands. "Here, drink! I'm sure you're thirsty, and a good cup of tea always lifts the spirits."

Tomás took a sip of the tea, then glanced around the room. "I actually released a soul?"

"I think so! Overheard Aelia talking to Teodozia—said one of you released a soul. When Teodozia asked who, Aelia said it, and I quote, 'was not the twins.' I knew you'd be able to do it!" Cevin reached for Tomás's hand, then stopped. He flushed.

*Potential...* Tomás recited to himself, recanting Aelia's comment. He locked eyes with Cevin. "I don't think I would have succeeded in this without you."

"Eh, I doubt that. You've got a lot of talent there, Tom."

"Yes, but without your help...I might have succumbed to the voices. I mean it, Cevin. Without you...I wouldn't have a constant." He reached for Cevin's hand and squeezed it. "You've been my constant."

Cevin's face reddened, "What...what do you mean by that?"

"I, uh..." Tomás fumbled. What did he mean? Cevin had always been there for him, but now...it felt like more.

*We have potential.*

"Well, I, um," Tomás continued to stammer. "It means that, um... Well—"

Cevin cut him off, planting a light kiss on his lips. Tomás's entire body froze. It was brief but intimate. It silenced any threat of voices and reassured him that peace was within his reach.

Then, Cevin pulled away, stumbling a few paces backward. He threw his hands up as he paced away from Tomás. "Tom, I'm sorry. I... Well... Sorry!"

Tomás went to speak, but before any words escaped, Cevin fled the room.

He stumbled from the bed, ready to chase after Cevin, only for the door to open again moments later.

But Cevin did not return.

Instead, Aelia meandered into the room. Upon seeing Tomás, she cocked her head to the side, her lips curved upwards in an ever-so-slight smile.

"I was about to wake you, Ívar, and Elva. But I am glad to see you up and about, Tomás."

Tomás lowered his head, "I am sorry if I impeded your plans."

"Oh, not at all. I am taking you, Ívar, and Elva onto the Schanifeld. You need more practice if you are to be as successful as your counterparts."

Tomás shuffled. "Did I not perform a release properly?"

"No, you did well... but you must practice. A Mist Keeper's duty is to release countless souls every day. If you are to succumb to exhaustion after each performance, you will not be a successful Mist Keeper."

Tomás opened his mouth to object but stopped himself.

"Now, once Ívar and Elva have awoken, we will go. I'll have Teodozia bring you food in the meantime. Nourishment is imperative."

She glided over to Ívar and Elva, leaving Tomás standing there with that punctuated statement and no chance to reconcile the haunting kiss on his lips.

Aelia kept them out in the Schanifeld for three days, guiding them through the Mist to old and new burial sites.

With each release, Tomás's head spun with voices, their languages solidifying as if he knew them his whole life. For the first few releases, he collapsed, spiraling into disorientation. But, by the end of the second day, he performed each release with ease and comfort.

Ívar and Elva soon caught up, performing their releases while sharing in laughter. Tomás kept to himself, though, his thoughts locked on Cevin whenever he had a fleeting moment. That kiss, however brief, lingered on his lips. He couldn't shake it. Romance had always been something to allude to him. Back in the La Catedral, he never even considered it.

Only when he met Varden did he learn kindness.

And now, with Cevin, he'd learned love.

When he closed his eyes, Tomás didn't hear the voices. Instead, he saw Cevin's face, with that awkward-shaped lip and wide smile.

Aelia did not offer any compliments or pride over Tomás's success. But, as she led them back into the Phrontistery, she seemed to almost fly across the Mist, guided by confidence and pride.

As usual, Tomás did not join the others in the dining hall, retiring to his room to change into fresh clothes.

His heart stammered as he neared the door to his room. Sweat glossed over his hands as he touched the doorknob.

But the room was empty. On the bed, a fresh set of clothes sat folded on the bed, with a pile of parchment paper on top.

Tomás picked the first piece up and read it to himself, slowly sounding out each letter.

*Tom—*

*I wrote down everything you missed while you were gone.*

*I am sorry for what happened in the infirmary. It was a momentary lapse in emotions. I hope we can forget and continue our friendship.*

*-Cev*

Tomás stared at the note, reading through it once more. "I don't want to pretend it never happened," Tomás said aloud. "It was all I thought about when I was gone..."

"Do you mean that?"

Tomás spun around. Cevin stood in the doorway.

"I, um, knew when you returned when you touched my note. I could feel it." Cevin scuffed his shoes on the ground, shrinking in on himself.

Tomás placed the paper back on the bed and approached Cevin. With a trembling hand, he cupped Cevin's cheek, holding it for a moment...

Before returning Cevin's kiss.

# ELEVEN

F inally, Tomás felt as though he belonged.

It was a strange feeling, like a warmth settling in his core. But he understood his voices, he completed a release, and he had found his constant.

While the voices still bickered in his head, if he focused on Cevin's uneven smile, or the spark in his silver eyes, Tomás felt like the voices were just a bit quieter. He even focused on his lessons, recanting history without hinderance, and hanging onto every warning of war.

The talk of war became more apparent; while details remained locked behind a veil of mystery, that not even the voices could break, Aelia and Teodozia constantly spoke about Ningursu's feud with Tehuti Kek. Every time, they glossed over the details of the actual war, only that the horrors grew with each passing day.

"Why do they not give us any details on this dispute?" Tomás asked Cevin as they sat together on the bed.

Cevin glanced up from the papers on his lap. His frantic writing to his sister highlighted the page, sloppy and difficult to decipher. "It is strange. Whenever I try to...peak into their conversations, it's like smoke."

"Surely knowledge would allow us to be better prepared."

"Unfortunately, Ningursu is one to keep secrets."

"I cannot help but wonder if he is real..." Tomás trailed off. What was this strange person like? Tomás almost pictured a giant, taller than Varden, towering over everyone.

A God in his own right.

"I met him once. Briefly. He is real." Cevin folded his piece of paper, then turned to Tomás. "I am sure we will get our answers soon. We cannot be kept in the dark forever."

But, as the rumors continued, questions grew. While Tomás and Cevin remained quiet, others gathered around Teodozia during dinner whenever Aelia was not present.

"What is he like?" a mousy disciple asked one day.

"Who?" Teodozia asked, her eyes heavy.

"Ningursu!"

Teodozia took another bite of her food, then said, "You shall meet him soon."

Ívar interjected, "You always say that!"

"It is all I can say."

*He is not as impressive as one might think.* Teodozia's voice whispered in Tomás's ear.

He showed no sign of hearing it, keeping his head lowered. While other questions filled the rest of the evening, he and Cevin were the first to leave.

With their hands laced together, they cuddled on the bed, staring at Cevin's messy side of the room.

"Do you suppose I should clean? I doubt I'll finish half those letters. "Cevin asked.

"Letters?"

"To my sister. I used to write to her all the time, telling her of my discoveries. But...I have been distracted. I'm sure it would be better if I cleaned."

"It doesn't bother me either way... if it gives you peace."

"Hm."

Tomás glanced at Cevin, "Really, I do not have any qualms. You are who you are."

"You always notice things like that."

"I hear voices."

"You read minds."

"Which is odd to say...as I have never been a good reader."

Cevin raised his brow, "You read all the time!"

Tomás fiddled with his fingers before finally confessing, "To teach myself. I only learned to read on the voyage here."

"Really?"

"Yes."

"Well, I learn more about you every day, Tom." Cevin laughed. "I s'pose you were too busy reading others to understand words."

"Perhaps."

"You are always reading 'em. Even at dinner, you were reading," Cevin continued. "I saw you watching Teodozia."

"She was talking."

"Not because of that. You were understanding her. I was, too. She was clearly tired."

"She did seem exhausted..."

"What was she thinking?"

"Just that we wouldn't be impressed with Ningursu. I tried not to listen much else, though..." Tomás crossed his legs and frowned. "It feels disrespectful to listen."

"But it is your magic, and it is fantastic."

"It is an intrusion of privacy."

"But what if I give you permission?" Cevin asked.

"That's different."

"Then what am I thinking?" Cevin smirked.

Tomás raised his eyebrow, then grinned. *The voice issued a single command, one he was willing to follow.*

*Stop moping and kiss me.*

So, it continued.

Lessons.

Releases.

Constantly.

All until the snow once again came and went.

When the first sign of white flowers peaked through the snow, Aelia summoned the class into the grand hall, a cloak of Mist following behind her.

Tomás and Cevin gathered in the back of the room, gripping each other's hands. The smoke rose and fell around them. Tomás's first thought went to Ningursu.

But Aelia destroyed that inclination at once.

"Today, you will be here to witness as one of our own joins the ranks of Mist Keeper." Aelia said, "Teodozia has been training for many years, and she guided many of you. Now, she will finally reach her true potential."

Hushed whispers fell over the room. Their voices echoed.

*Finally!*

*I am sure Teodozia will do amazing.*

*Oh! This is fantastic!*

Cevin squeezed Tomás's hand, his own voice whispering, *It will be okay.*

Tomás grimaced and returned his attention to Aelia.

"Teodozia is preparing now. She will join us momentarily. For now, please take a seat along the wall," Aelia said.

They all obliged, waiting. For everyone else, the room would be silent. But their voices overlapped, clawing in Tomás's ears.

He tightened his grip around Cevin's hand.

*Focus on me,* Cevin's voice whispered.

So Tomás obliged, tracing the grooves of Cevin's hand and keeping his gaze locked on the center of the room.

A few minutes passed before the doors opened. Teodozia walked in, her brown hair pulled back, a long black cloak covering her body. Smoke gathered at her feet, pulsating with each breath. No one spoke.

But for a single voice.

*I am not ready.*

Tomás stared at Teodozia as she walked past, brushing smoke along Tomás's face. Despite her thoughts, her face remained calm, a callous mask plastered over her dark eyes.

She approached Aelia.

"You have made me quite proud, Teodozia," Aelia smiled at Teodozia. It was a strange smile, forced in a way, barely revealing her teeth. "All these years of hard work... and here you are, more than capable to be a full Mist Keeper."

"I am honored, Lady Aelia," Teodozia bowed her head.

"Ningursu wanted to be here, but unfortunately, more pressing matters caught his attention. He will meet you once you have joined us, though, ready to harness the Mist together. For now, it is time."

Aelia removed a small vial from her pocket. She uncorked it, letting a strange silver liquid bubble to the surface. Then, with the smoke gathering at her fingertips, she shook the vial once. There, it darkened to a steel gray.

She handed it to Teodozia, then nodded.

Teodozia stared at the vial, frowning. Tomás couldn't read her thoughts, as if a wall had gone up around her.

A beat passed.

Then, with her eyes shut, Teodozia raised the vial to her lips.

Almost as soon as the liquid entered her mouth.

Nothing happened for a moment.

But a twitch.

Then stumble.

And a collapse.

With one final breath before she ceased.

Another pause.

Followed by a uniform, shocked gasp.

Before the questions began, Aelia put her hand up, silencing the room.

Where it stayed, like a half-exhaled breath.

Waiting...

Hoping...

Until the smoke rose around Teodozia's body.

It swirled in circles, capturing Teodozia's limbs and body, sifting through the floors and walls. It danced at Aelia's feet and waltzed between each of the students. Tomás shuddered as a wave came over him.

"Look!" Cevin tugged at Tomás's arm.

Out of the smoke, a figure emerged. Similar in height to Teodozia, it teetered just where her body had once lay. The Mist structured itself around her face and limbs, pulling Teodozia back to life.

But it wasn't life.

No...she was dead.

But not just dead.

A Mist Keeper.

Tomás almost smiled.

Then, as the Mist settled, Teodozia's voice returned.

But it wasn't even her voice. Or a thought.

Rather, it was a scream.

It began in Tomás's head, ringing like an obnoxious bell. As he raised his hands to his ears, the voice became real, echoing from the mist. It tugged at the air, reaching across the entire hall, yanking at everyone.

The figure in the Mist convulsed, collapsing again to the ground like the body.

The screaming did not stop.

"What's happening?" Tomás asked Cevin.

Cevin stared, eyes wide, his bottom lip quivering.

"Cevin!? What is wrong?" Tomás tugged at Cevin's arm.

Before anyone answered, Aelia's voice rang out, "Everyone leave...now!"

Even if Tomás resisted, there was no choice offered. Like a tsunami, the Mist pushed everyone from the room, locking the door as the last student stumbled into the corridor.

# TWELVE

Aelia locked them in the bunkrooms for a week, allowing them out only to use the lavatory. Unassuming ghosts delivered food, providing no updates or talk. While Tomás tried to search for voices that might provide an answer, nothing blessed him with clarity.

But the voices were not the only thing that had fallen silent. Cevin had retreated into silence, his eyes heavy and face pale. He scribbled on parchment, writing half-finished letters to his sister, before chucking the papers at the wall and hiding beneath his covers. With few words exchanged, all Tomás could do was sit with him, providing the same comfort that Cevin once provided him.

As the week ended, Cevin's behavior changed. He approached Tomás, holding a letter in his hands.

"Tom…" he whispered.

Tomás wanted more than anything to swoop Cevin into his arms, celebrating the end to silence. But he knew better, maintaining his composure.

"Yes?"

"Could you read this letter to Edith? I want to make sure it is sound…" Cevin handed the paper to him.

Tomás blinked a few times, taking in the words. Written in Cevin's native tongue, he let the surrounding Mist translate the words and read.

*Dearest Edith,*

*I hope this letter finds you in pleasant spirits. While I apologize for not writing recently, it is not without cause. As I told you, training to be a Mist Keeper is hard work that often leaves me drained. But worry not - I still have companionship in Tom. Loneliness is one qualm that I do not fear.*

*But I do have a fear now: Death. If you recall, to become one with the Mist, I must abandon my living breath. That had never terrified me before… but I just witnessed one of my peers enter the Mist. It did not go as intended.*

*As she attempted to join the Mist, her senses overwhelmed me. It was as if she was blind, wandering in darkness, while the world burned around her. Noises held no definition, and even the air tasted sour. The pain was beyond my wildest nightmares. Imagine being skinned alive, both inside and out.*

*I was only receiving a hint of that pain, enough where I could hide it from watching eyes. But... I fear that pain now more than anything. What if I cannot push it away?*

*Edith, I tell you this only because I am scared. I will keep working, of course, just as I promised you. But please, give me some of your strength. You are the strongest person I know.*

*I look forward to your letter.*

*Your brother,*
*Cevin.*

Tomás read over the letter, sweat gathering at his fingertips. As he finished the last word, he met Cevin's eyes. He croaked, "So you *felt* what Teodozia was going through then..."

"I have been processing it," Cevin whispered.

"Oh, Cev." Tomás placed the letter on the bed and took Cevin's hands. "I am sorry you felt such pain. You should have told me sooner. I am here."

"I know. I just worry for you. I don't want to see you suffer like that when the time comes."

"And I do not wish to see you under the same fate."

Cevin squeezed Tomás's hands, "We must do better. For Teodozia."

"How?"

"By continuing to learn...together."

"Together," Tomás recited, then pulled Cevin close. Alone, no one would cross into the Mist. But together, even the weakest could become gods.

# Thirteen

Aelia left without addressing what happened to Teodozia, placing Estefano, the second oldest, in charge of the Phrontistery. Lessons returned to the classroom, where they recanted the different types of Mist and quizzed the disciples on their magic and abilities. War became a frequent conversation but without substance. It was the same circular conversation, warning that the balance between Life and Death had been compromised.

Cevin returned to his usual, smiling self, especially after one of the ghosts delivered a letter from his sister. His smile returned while reading it. Yet, there remained a sad glimmer in his eyes. Tomás did all he could to help Cevin. Constant thoughts of worry and despair crossed over Cevin's mind. Tomás took each one and stored them in his heart.

Without Teodozia, without Aelia, the seasons changed. With spring upon them, Tomás made time to venture outside with Cevin, away from the voices and the questions. Some days, they sat by the sea, watching as ships bobbed in the distance. Tomás often wondered what became of Varden and his crew. But no familiar faces or ships docked in port.

"I just can't figure out how Teodozia failed," Cevin said one day as they returned to the Phrontistery. "She knew everything about being a Mist Keeper. And with her magic, it was like she understood everything."

Tomás furrowed his brow. They continued to walk along, the white flowers waving in the distance. If he focused long enough, the voices started to whisper, repeating over and over again. The words were different for each person, a fleeting final thought before their death. If he followed them, then he might release their souls.

"Maybe," Tomás recited, "maybe she failed because she didn't master what it meant to be a Mist Keeper."

Cevin cocked his head to the side. "What do you mean, Tom?"

"It might not be the same for everyone, but for me... if I'm going to be confident in being a Mist Keeper, then I should be confident in my duties as a Mist Keeper… and be confident that the voices won't mislead me. That starts with releasing souls."

Cevin followed Tomás's gaze out at the field. "Teodozia was always busy teaching us… rather than *being* a Mist Keeper."

"So, we should practice releases on our own time then, right?" Tomás took Cevin's hands.

"We're not allowed—"

"But we want to succeed and… I want us to succeed together. I cannot succeed without you by my side."

Cevin's eyes fell, then he nodded.

"So, you'll release souls with me?" Tomás asked.

The response was a whisper as fleeting as the kiss that followed, "Constantly."

# FOURTEEN

In the early mornings and late evenings, Tomás and Cevin ventured into the Schanifeld. They conducted releases of bodies trapped beneath the flowers, homing in on their craft in a shared silence. They met souls once entrapped in war, souls that fled from homes, souls that went for a walk and met their match, and many more. Each bore a story, laced in the thoughts that Tomás captured with each release. He and Cevin never said much about their individual release, wearing the burden of the dead close to their chests. But in the evening, back in their room, they shared a space on the bed, holding each other in silent reflection.

As they released more souls, their magic grew, allowing them to transverse the Mist across the Schanifeld and back, releasing souls far away from the Phrontistery.

This continued well into winter. No one knew when Aelia might return, locking the disciples in a permanent state of study.

Until one morning, upon entering the dining hall, Tomás found a familiar bearded face.

There, sitting at the head of the table, was that strange man from the cathedral years earlier. Tomás had the crisp cut of his beard, his long curly hair, and hauntingly silver eyes committed to memory.

Cevin gasped beside Tomás, his thought fleeting. *That's Ningursu!*

Tomás's chest tightened. Was he really the legendary Ningursu, the one who created the Mist Keepers of his own accord?

Before he asked Cevin, Aelia emerged from the veil of Mist behind Ningursu. "Everyone, please take a seat."

Tomás took a seat next to Cevin. No one spoke as Ningursu bore down on them, his silver eyes reaching into their very souls.

Silence tapped.

Waited.

Sang.

Finally, Ningursu spoke, his voice like molten lava. "I am overjoyed that I finally found time to visit with all of you, my disciples. My name is Ningursu, as I am sure most of you have inferred. You have heard much about me, but I have yet to meet many of you."

No one spoke. Even if Tomás wanted to speak, it was as though his voice had been stolen.

"In due time, I will spend time with each of you. With the war mounting, I am quite worried... especially after what happened with our dear Teodozia."

Cevin squeezed Tomás's hand under the table, but if any thought crossed his mind, Tomás did not hear it.

"While I cannot wait to meet each of you, it is imperative that you understand the importance of your role... especially in the war that has been brewing for over a century." Ningursu rose, pacing around the room as he spoke. "While you have learned much of this war, with immortal magic users infringing on the rights of Life and Death. But I fear we may not have much time left before they finally destroy the balance for good." Ningursu turned to the window. "I have received insight that the leader of this palaver of immortals, Tehuti Kek, intends to expand their supply of In Domumus Divitiae. This will allow them to recruit countless individuals to their ranks, showing them that Death can be defeated. But that very rationale threatens the balance of the world." Ningursu turned back to the room. "I believe we need to come together as a unified Council of Custocaligo, or Mist

Keepers as the term you have adopted, for lack of a better descriptor. That is why I am here."

No one spoke, still watching Ningursu in awe. For someone as powerful as a God, it was strange to see this man. Other than his command of words and the smoke tossing around him, he was... Well, normal. He wasn't as tall as a giant or even as glamorous as the stars. At his core, Ningursu was a person.

Aelia spoke next, "After Teodozia's upsetting failure, I sought Ningursu. We agreed it was imperative that he assisted in your training. Starting tomorrow, each of you will sit with him so he can determine where in our Council you belong. Some of you will serve as warriors, fighting this foe. But others, you will maintain balance, releasing souls and conducting other duties. Your role in all of this will be at Ningursu's discretion. Until then, consider both futures and how you see yourself in this Council."

Hushed whispers fell over the room. Tomás squeezed Cevin's hand.

Death had arrived.

And he had set a deadline.


Tomás and Cevin didn't release souls that evening. Instead, they took a seat outside the fortress, where the moon cast its silver light. Once again, they sat in a comfortable silence. There was no need to discuss Ningursu. Just like Cevin sensed Tomás's nerves, Tomás heard Cevin's own concerns.

For now, they had each other.

Constantly.

Different voices echoed across the front of Tomás's mind. He had gotten better at ignoring them, pushing them to the back of his thoughts so he could focus on the present. Time was better spent listening to Cevin's gentle breaths, tracing the insides of his palm, or observing the wind going through his hair.

If he had to live an eternity as a Mist Keeper, at least he would have Cevin by his side. He could live forever in the moment if Cevin was his guide.

That was a promise Tomás made to himself.

Constantly.

And with Cevin, the nerves that captured the word "forever" disappeared. Together. Constantly. Forever.

Forever…

*No more.*

Tomás's trance broke. The voice did not roar through his head but whispered. It didn't belong to Cevin. Had he opened his mind to another student? It didn't sound like anyone else.

*No more!*

The voice was louder this time.

*No! More!*

It wasn't just loud; it was shrieking, like a child trapped in a cage.

*No. Not a child.*

*NO!*

It was familiar. So familiar.

*NO!*

Tomás sat up. "Teodozia?"

Cevin eyed him. "What're you goin' on about?"

And with Cevin's question, the distressed voice ceased.

Tomás blinked a few times, then wiped his eyes. Tears fell down his cheeks.

"Tom?" Cevin pressured.

He shook his head. "I… I thought I heard… her voice… Teodozia's voice. I thought…"

Cevin raised his brow. "I don't feel her."

"But I… I heard… I thought…"

Cevin pulled Tomás into his arms. With his head on Cevin's chest, Tomás listened to his heartbeat, counting each thud while gripping Cevin's hands.

"She's gone," Cevin whispered.

"I know. I just… yes, I know," Tomás inhaled. "I know."

"We're going to be a'ight. You and I have been practicing… we won't end up like Teodozia."

"Promise?" Tomás met Cevin's gaze. "Constantly."

# Fifteen

Ningursu summoned Cevin first thing the next morning, leaving Tomás to traverse through the day, still fixated on Teodozia's voice. It hadn't returned, even as he willed the voices to him at mealtime. Had he simply imagined it? Was it a voice out in the white flowers, begging to be released? Or was it another student that he'd mistaken for Teodozia?

It had been so vivid. So real.

But Teodozia was gone.

And Tomás swore he wouldn't be next.

After the evening meal, Tomás returned to the fields of white flowers and released three more souls. It had become second nature to him at this point. With each released soul, his grasp of language grew stronger while his magic obeyed almost his every move. He needn't worry about succumbing to the voices again. Here, with the souls of the dead, he was truly a Mist Keeper.

It was with this reminder that he returned to his bunk.

Cevin greeted him at the door, throwing his arms around Tomás and kissing him full on the lips.

"What was that for?" Tomás laughed as Cevin pulled him into the room.

"Tom! I have so much to tell you, let me say!" The excitement in his step, the glisten in his eyes, it reminded Tomás of when he first met Cevin.

"Oh?" Tomás asked, smirking as he took a seat next to Cevin.

"Let me tell you, Ningursu is one of the nicest people I have spoken to in a long while. He is sincere—mysterious, yes, but sincere—and he really listened to all my concerns. We were wrong to be so nervous around him."

Cevin's excitement bled into Tomás, and he smiled.

"He and I spoke for hours. I showed him what my magic does...and guess what he told me? He said that I remind him of a younger version of himself! Me! He thinks I have much potential, and he wants to work on growing my powers. Me! Can you believe it, Tom? Oh, I'll need to write Edith... but Tom! I cannot believe it!"

Tomás's grin expanded. "I can believe it. I always knew you were fantastic."

"Yes, but…me? Tom—I can't even fathom it. I'm still giddy. Feel my hands. They're shaking!"

Tomás gripped Cevin's trembling hands, unable to tear his attention away from the joy radiating from Cevin's face.

Cevin continued his rambling, "I am sure he'll be just as impressed as with you, Tom. You have come so far, and if he thought I was interesting, wait until he—"

Tomás placed a finger over Cevin's lips. "Shush."

"But Tom—"

"Tonight, we celebrate you," Tomás said.

Before Cevin started another tirade, Tomás planted a kiss on his forehead, then continued to move his lips down Cevin's face, neck, and body.

It took a fortnight for Ningursu to summon Tomás. In that time, Cevin's excitement reignited, his laughter once again booming, and the light sparkling in his eyes. Tomás admired Cevin's happiness. He loved Cevin at his best and worst, but this version was the one Tomás adored. Confident Cevin. Kind Cevin. Jubilant Cevin. He couldn't wait until they had time alone in the evenings to touch and kiss after they practiced their releases and lessons for the day.

But Cevin couldn't join him as he walked the narrow stairwell of the north tower to Ningursu's private suite. Despite Cevin's reassurance, Tomás's hands quivered as he knocked on the door. His stomach flipped over, waiting for the knob to turn. As the door creaked open, his head spun.

On the other side stood Ningursu, smiling.

"Ah, Tomás. Please, join me. I am excited to hear what you've accomplished since our last encounter." Ningursu motioned for him into the room. Along the walls stood towering shelves decorated with artifacts, jewels, papers, and books. Three chairs gathered around a basin in the center of the room, bubbling with strange silver liquid. Ningursu motioned for Tomás to sit in the chair, covering the basin with a wooden lid before taking a set down himself.

"Go on. Do not be afraid, Tomás. I am here to help."

Tomás licked his lip, then asked, "Why didn't you tell me who you were?"

"Would you have believed me at the time?"

"I...suppose not." Tomás did not make eye contact with Ningursu.

"That is why I kept myself anonymous, as I am sure you understand now. I was concerned for you at first...but you have certainly grown in both mind and power. You aren't the same boy I met in El Limra."

"I've been learning," Tomás replied.

"And what have you learned about yourself?"

Tomás crossed his legs and picked at the cuff of his shirt, brushing his fingers over the small piece of Varden's cloak. He hadn't needed it recently, but it was still there, always on his wrist". He replied with care, "The voices I hear... They are actually the thoughts of others. I can use those thoughts to release souls."

"Is that all?"

Tomás nodded.

"I see." Ningursu said nothing else for a minute. He ran his fingers through his beard, attention locked on Tomás. With each second, the Mist rose around them, masking the shelves and walls, so Tomás only sat there with Ningursu.

But just as soon as the Mist rose, it fell again, like a blink of an eye.

"I believe there is much more to your magic than you have uncovered. If you can hear, who is to say you cannot speak in someone's head? A message, after all, goes two ways."

Tomás hadn't thought of that. The voices never replied to him before... why bother speaking to them?

"Let us practice. I shall temporarily part the Mist so that you may touch my thoughts. When you hear them, try to respond. Imagine that you are... climbing on these wisps of Mist, fluttering about the room, screaming. Then you might be able to respond back." Ningursu said as he reached across, taking Tomás's hand in his icy hands. "Go on, my boy, try."

Tomás swallowed, then turned his attention to Ningursu. The voices remained quiet at first. Then, muffled through the smoke, the voices began their hum. At the forefront, Ningursu's voice echoed.

*Tomás, follow the voice. If you can hear it, respond with your favorite color.*

Favorite color? Tomás had never even chosen a favorite color. But as he pictured the Mist before him, parting like a funnel so that he could shout back, he chose the first color that entered his mind.

*Silver.* He responded. Then, under his breath, he whispered, "Like Cevin's eyes."

Ningursu smirked. *Very good.*

Then, the barriers went up around Ningursu's mind again, and the voices rescinded into the Mist.

# SIXTEEN

Tomás and Cevin shared their mutual excitement that evening. After all, Cevin was right - Ningursu wanted what was best for them. Giddiness filled Tomás at the mere prospect; it was more than just voices! Everyone's mind was his canvas, and if he harnessed his abilities correctly, then nothing would be impossible!

The excitement followed them into the morning, where the other disciples babbled around the table. This newfound exuberance filled the room. Even Tomás couldn't help but smile.

As Ningursu walked into the room, the commotion ceased. He took to the front of the room with a smile. With smoke gathering around him, there was almost something otherworldly about him.

Like a God.

A true Mist Keeper.

His voice rumbled as he spoke, "All of you have remarkable talents, and I believe each of you will serve an important role in the success of our coalition of Mist Keepers. But I have selected a handful of you whom I believe will benefit from additional lessons with me due to the very nature of your magic. So, if I call your name, please come forward... the first lesson will begin today."

Tomás glanced at Cevin, whose eyes had widened with anticipation.

"Can Elva, Estefano, Imelda, and Cevin come with me?" Ningursu asked.

Cevin's lips twitched, forming a slight smile. As he met Tomás's eyes, though, his face fell.

*I could have sworn you'd be chosen,* Cevin thought.

Tomás squeezed his hand. *Go.*

Cevin stared at Tomás.

*Can you hear me?* Tomás forced his thoughts forward again.

Cevin nodded.

Now, it was Tomás's turn to smile.

Like a receding tide, Cevin released Tomás's hand. They shared one last glance before Cevin approached Ningursu and the others.

You'll do fantastic, Tomás thought. If Cevin heard, he didn't show as he left the room with Ningursu.

It was strange not having Cevin by his side through the day's lessons. Tomás had grown accustomed to Cevin's thoughts scratching the back of his mind. Instead, the lulling frustrations of the other students echoed. Tomás didn't share in the disappointment; he wasn't sure if he wanted to be Ningursu's focus. He preferred focusing on releases and finding his own path to strengthen his magic.

After the daily lessons repeating the same historical tales, Tomás ventured out into the Schanifeld to release souls, moving through the motions as if he were already a Mist Keeper in full. All he wanted was to provide guidance to these lost souls. Wasn't that the purpose of a Mist Keeper? Not to master ridiculous magic but to help.

To grow.

To be a constant guide.

And to pacify the dead.

So, he returned to the Phrontistery as night finally fell with that very goal still vibrating in his heart...so loud that he almost didn't hear the voice scratching the back of his mind.

*No more. Please!*

Tomás paused in the stairwell.

*Please. Please...no more.*

Tomás glanced around the empty stairwell. Rather than heading down to his bunk, he took another step up the stairs.

The voice grew louder.

*It hurts. No more... please.*

He gathered his own thoughts at the front of his mind, taking another step up the stairs. *Teodozia? Is that you?*

The voice did not respond.

*Teodozia?*

Another pause.

Then, a whisper. *Tomás...*

*Where are you, Teodozia?*

*Darkness.*

*Darkness?*

*Darkness.*

*What does that mean?*

If Teodozia replied, Tomás didn't hear. Footsteps echoed from up the stairwell, dancing with muffled voices. As a shadow flickered on the wall, Tomás hurried back down the stairs to his quiet bunk where no one waited.

# SEVENTEEN

For the next few days, Cevin returned to their bunk late in the evening, leaving Tomás with no time to bring up Teodozia. He hoped to tell Cevin each morning, but by the time the sun rose, the space beside him was already empty.

So Tomás continued his routine. He practiced his releases in secret while attending the otherwise repetitive lessons about the history of Mist Keepers, the dynamics of languages, and the strength of the Mist. As his interest in the lessons fell, his mind wandered, locking onto the constant moaning of Teodozia.

Or, what sounded like her.

He hadn't found a chance to ascend the stairwell. Whenever he dared sneak up a few paces, shadows danced along the wall, preventing him from exploring the rooms at the top of the tower.

After nearly a week passed, Tomás woke to find Cevin still asleep in bed. He planted a kiss on Cevin's forehead and brushed the dusty blonde hair from his face.

Cevin stirred.

"Do you want me to get you breakfast, Cev?" Tomás asked.

Cevin opened his eyes and smiled. "Let me look at you first," he murmured.

Tomás clenched Cevin's hands, letting his gaze settle. They held each other there for a moment.

"Ningursu has been keeping us busy… I feel like I haven't seen you in a year," Cevin said.

"It has been a week… and there is much I'd like to talk about."

"I do, too. Today, I have all the time."

"Really?"

"Yes. Ningursu is letting us rest today, as tomorrow, he and Aelia are taking us for further practice. He wants to test our limits…see if we can face the foes awaiting us on the battlefield. We have to be able to match their magic."

"So, you are leaving tomorrow? For how long?"

"He didn't say…just that he's leaving Loukios in charge again."

"I see…" Tomás pondered.

"What are you thinking, Tomás?" Cevin remarked.

Tomás chose his words carefully, "I've been... hearing Teodozia more. Every time I try to find her, Aelia or someone else is in the tower. Now... I might be able to see for myself."

"Are you sure it's her?" Cevin asked.

"Not quite... but I have to find out."

Cevin reached for Tomás's cheek, running his finger over the stubble on his chin. "Be careful, Tom. If it is Teodozia, we do not know what has become of her."

"If you are worried, I give you permission to see through my eyes when you need. My senses are yours, my body is yours, and my mind is yours. Constantly."

"As is mine. Constantly and forever," Cevin pulled Tomás into a kiss where they could be just that; together - mind, body, and soul.

# EIGHTEEN

A heaviness hung in Tomás's chest as Cevin left the next day. The uncertainty of his return created a void, one that Tomás could not fill as he meandered through his day. He paid little attention to his lessons, and even his releases proved to be forgettable.

It wasn't until evening fell and he returned to the tower that his sense of self returned. He paused, staring up at the stairwell. With Aelia and Ningursu gone, now was the perfect time.

But Teodozia's voice didn't beckon him.

So instead, he returned to his empty quarters and lay beneath the blankets, holding onto the tattered piece of his cloak and one of Cevin's many notes.

For the following days, Tomás did not hear Teodozia. Perhaps it had all been in his head? Or maybe she left with

Aelia and Ningursu to train with the others. But if that was the case, then why hide her? Why pretend she had failed in becoming a Mist Keeper?

He couldn't shake the questions as the days passed. Without Cevin to quell them, they grew louder, echoing almost like the voices that trapped him for many years. Whenever evening came, he paused at the stairs, pondering the voyage to the top of the tower.

But he did not ascend them until a fortnight passed, and whispers crawled into his head as he returned to the tower.

*Water...*

He focused on the stairs.

*Water. So thirsty.* The voice said again.

*Teodozia?* Tomás thought. *Is that you?*

The voice responded, *Please, water.*

Tomás swallowed and glanced over his shoulder. None of the other disciples loitered in the stairwell. Sweat gathered in his palms as he climbed the stairs.

*Bring me water. Please. So thirsty.*

The stairs creaked as he climbed, twisting around the tower, past the second floor, and into the narrow wall walk. Small slit windows cast a dusky orange glow over the stairs. As the stairs twisted, they narrowed, forming a path big enough for only one person at a time.

Then, the stairs suddenly stopped, hitting the ceiling with no warning. Tomás ducked, pressing his hand to the ceiling.

*Parched.* The voice was almost right beside Tomás. But where?

He felt along the wall and up along the ceiling. The stone and wood did not harbor any abnormalities. He frowned as he tapped them. Was there a sort of magic hiding Teodozia from him?

Nothing moved.

He took a few steps backward to get a better look, stumbling slightly as he found his footing. One step was slightly off balance, its wood popping ever-so-slightly up from the nails. Tomás kicked it with the tip of his shoe.

The step lifted from its spot, and with it, the other three steps above it shifted, revealing an opening. Smoke pooled from it, wreaking of rotting eggs.

Tomás glanced over his shoulder, then stepped through the doorway.

The room beyond it was dark, with smoke continuing to dance along the walls. He squinted, only a sliver of light entering from the stairwell.

There, a figure hunched over in the darkness, with chains latched to their wrists and ankles.

*Help me...* The voice boomed in Tomás's head.

He took another step toward the figure. "Teodozia? Is that you?"

The figure raised its head.

But it wasn't Teodozia.

Sure, it had her face, but there was something... wrong with it. Her eyes, once silver, now glowed yellow. The hair on her head had grayed, while the skin clinging to her bones looked more like paper. With every breath, smoke rippled through her. It waltzed through the air, wrapping around Tomás.

Suffocating...

Dragging...

As though he was drowning in a sea of voices. Alone.

Without identity.

Without self.

Without his constant.

*Help me!* Teodozia's voice rang again.

Tomás stumbled backward and out of the room. Another voice crawled into his head. From whom? It wasn't clear. But its words rang as he pulled the hidden doorway shut.

*She's a monster. A failure. Lock her away.*

*Never return.*

*Forget Teodozia.*

# NINETEEN

Over the next few weeks, Tomás drowned himself in his own lessons, ignoring whatever that *thing* was in the tower. Perhaps it was once Teodozia... but now... he couldn't be sure. Is that what failing did to Mist Keepers? Did they become something else?

When he closed his eyes, he pictured her, with her lopsided jaw and glowing eyes. The smoke erupted from her like a volcano, and with every plume, another fear bubbled to the surface.

The voices grew louder.

And all Tomás could do was flee.

So, he fled from his problems and spent countless hours in the Schanifeld, releasing souls and waiting for Cevin to return home from his training—although the time between each return grew longer and longer.

Each evening, he scanned through Cevin's old notes from class, imaging his constant next to him, reading along with him or scribbling away at letters to his sister. Yet, his imagination could not cure the loneliness in his heart, further scarred by the stacks of notes Cevin received from his sister.

While the fortress bustled with lessons and smoky ghosts, Tomás retreated into loneliness, accepting it as the only sanctuary. Alone, the voices wouldn't haunt him.

Alone, Teodozia might finally disappear.

So, he continued his routine and waited for Cevin while counting the passing days. Every day that Cevin wasn't there, the sky grew darker, and worries grew more constant. This silent war brewing on the horizon lingered. Was Cevin fighting in it now? Was the foe nearing?

Sometimes, Tomás couldn't help but wonder if it was merely a story, composed by Ningursu and Aelia to motivate the disciples to continue their training.

But the few times Cevin returned highlighted that heightened sense of war. He would say little, crawling into the cot with Tomás, where they held each other for those brief nights. Tomás treasured those moments, but the training that Ningursu had put them through left Cevin tired. Even his thoughts echoed with the same exhaustion, and Tomás hadn't the chance to speak of Teodozia nor of the countless hours of training.

He accepted his new life, though, and with Cevin and the others missing for days, he chose his own adventures. It became a regular feat for Tomás to avoid his redundant lessons and venture into the Schanifeld for hours. He navigated through lost souls, letting their last thoughts dance across the top of his mind. No one asked where he went; they didn't seem to even care.

Except for the occasional voice coming from Teodozia, begging for him to help.

He lost track of the moons between Cevin's returns. Releasing souls blended like watercolors, and time was as fleeting as a passing thought. The seasons changed, and winter returned with a thick haze.

And from it, one crisp morning, emerged Ningursu, Aelia, and their entourage.

Tomás had returned from the Schanifeld upon seeing them, weary and broken, puffs of smoke fizzling like a dying flame. He slipped behind a wall as they approached, listening to their thoughts.

*I want to sleep.*

*This has to end.*

*Why did he take us there?*

As Cevin passed by, Tomás extended his thoughts, *Cev—what's going on?*

Cevin paused, then glanced in Tomás's direction. His thoughts raced over to Tomás. *They took us to Merton, where the Palaver of Immortals is. Ningursu wanted us to use our abilities to surprise them and end this war... but they were ready for us.*

*Are you okay?*

*Tired...but others were worse. Estefano lost an arm. Aelia tended to it, but it was horrid. So much blood. And then there was Elva...*

*Cev—*

*Ningursu will call a gathering soon. I'll meet you in the grand hall.*

The conversation fizzled. Tomás did not linger, hurrying back around the Phrontistery to the back entrance.

No one noticed as he entered the Grand Hall. Word of Ningursu's arrival spread fast. He hadn't shown his face since he selected his entourage, not even when the others returned. Questions sat in the air... Why had he returned so early in the day? What happened? What was next?

The questions, both vocally and internally, ceased as the grand doors swung open. Ningursu and Aelia entered, their cloaks tattered and skin marred by bruises, cuts, and cracks. Smoke pulsed in and out around their feet.

Behind them, the entourage of disciples filed into the room. Cevin locked eyes with Tomás. Blood vessels circled his pale iris. The permanent smile that sparkled in his eyes had vanished.

Tomás held back the urge to run to him, sharing that long, sorrowful gaze from afar.

It broke with Ningursu's voice. "Today is the day everything changes. Please, sit. We must act now, or the balance of Life and Death will be altered forever."

# TWENTY

Ningursu detailed the same story that Cevin shared with Tomás. His voice lacked excitement, his gray eyes solemn and distant. The Palaver of Immortals was growing, and if they did not work together, the entire Balance of Life and Death would forever change. Tomás kept his eyes locked on Cevin through the entire lecture, watching his dear friend's shoulders slump with each passing word. He couldn't imagine what Cevin saw there.

"I am also sorry to say that we have lost our dear Elva in this conquest," Ningursu said, turning his attention to her brother, "And I am especially sorry for you, Ívar."

Ívar's face paled. He opened his mouth, but no noise came out. Even his thoughts were silent.

Somehow, Elva's death was different compared to all the souls they released. Elva was a real person, someone they had trained with for years; now, they were gone.

"How?" Ívar whispered.

Yet Ningursu did not elaborate.

"How!?" Ívar demanded, louder this time.

"That is a story for another day," Ningursu said, then turned to Aelia beside him. Ívar continued to gawk, mouth ajar.

But Ningursu had moved on, turning back to the audience after sharing a single glance with his counterpart. "Aelia and I have weighed our options. We believe that to protect the sanctity of the...*Mist Keepers*, it is of utmost importance, you each complete your transition at once."

Murmurs fell over the room. Tomás's throat tightened.

But his questions were answered before they fully crossed his mind.

"I understand you saw Teodozia fail in her attempt to access her full potential. That is one reason I am here today - to ensure each of you succeed in your passage. We shall not let what happened to dear Teodozia happen to all of you; this is my promise."

Murmurs shook the room. Tomás couldn't make out the indistinct words, nor could he latch onto Cevin's soothing voice. Only one word slithered through, muffled and indistinct.

*That is not a promise you can keep.*

Ningursu turned to Aelia. "How long until it is ready?"

"Within the next hour."

"Good. Please retrieve it."

Aelia bowed her head, and then, with a plume of smoke, she vanished into the surrounding Mist.

"Now, everyone," Ningursu boomed. Smoke rose as he spoke, stitching its way into everyone's mouths. Tomás raised his hand to his lips. Try as he might, he couldn't pull them apart.

Ningursu continued, "I understand this is not how you each imagined this to occur. We hope to introduce our disciples into our world with grace. But the longer we wait, the more likely you are each at risk. You have each trained for many years, and I have faith in all of you. Do you not trust me?"

Everyone nodded in unison. But their thoughts told different tales.

*Of course we trust you.*

*You don't even know me; why should I trust you?*

*Teodozia failed... I certainly will.*

Tomás glanced in Cevin's direction again. Cevin's voice filled his mind, directed toward him.

*You've been training. I cannot imagine you failing.*

*Not as hard as you,* Tomás replied.

Cevin glanced over his shoulder and grimaced in Tomás's direction.

*Trust yourself, Tom. Just like I have constantly placed trust in you.*

*Constantly?*

*Constantly.*

# TWENTY-ONE

After Ningursu left the room, commotion and concern bustled around the room, highlighted by Ívar's wailing. Tomás rushed to Cevin's side, embracing him and sharing kisses over words.

*We are together now,* Tomás recited to himself, holding Cevin tight. He couldn't fathom what Cevin had experienced in the war. With so little mentioned, it was like a void of smoke, masking even the darkest hours.

And even if Tomás had wanted to ask, he wasn't given the time. Within minutes, Ningursu and Aelia returned, carrying a large basin. They positioned it at the front of the hall while the ghosts passed around wooden goblets to each of the disciples.

One at a time, Aelia motioned the disciples to the basin. She placed a gentle hand on Ívar's shoulder as he approached and whispered something that Tomás could not hear. Even if he tried to focus on the thoughts, the veil of Mist prevented his magic from working.

He was as lost as anyone.

But he had Cevin.

Together, they approached the basin. Tomás grasped his wooden goblet as he peered into the basin. Silver liquid, laced with strips of yellow and red, reflected at him. It twisted around the image of his face, and for one moment, he swore that the creature in the tower stared back at him.

The image disappeared as Cevin lowered his goblet into the basin.

Tomás did the same before returning to his spot against the far wall, with Cevin beside him, and the chatter around them hissing to a halt.

Once the last disciple filled their goblet, Ningursu stepped into the center of the room. He smiled, his silver eyes scanning each of them.

"It is time," he said. "With this mere drink, you will join us as full Mist Keepers—entwined with the Mist, neither alive nor dead. Together, you shall transcend into your full potential. So, I ask you all to take a moment to say your final prayers. Then, I shall instruct you to drink."

Tomás shared a glance with Cevin. They didn't need to speak. It all hung in the air: their friendship, their romance, and their constants.

As the last whispers of prayers echoed about the room, Ningursu raised a single hand. Smoke poured from his fingertips, and each piece wrapped around the disciples. Tomás's skin tingled as the smoke crossed it.

Then, as if tugged by a tether, his hands raised the goblet to his lips. Any thought of hesitation vanished from his mind.

He had to raise the goblet to his lips.

It was his sole duty.

He had no other choice.

His lips touched the brim of the goblet. He tilted it back and took a sip.

The strange liquid sizzled at his lips and slid over his tongue, down into his throat.

He blinked once.

But his vision already fizzled, nothing but specks of white filling his field of view.

No thoughts.

No breath.

Just one fleeting statement.

*Good luck, my constant.*

# TWENTY-TWO

The tethers snapped.
And so, he stood.
Alone.
With echoes.
Pounding...
Shouting...
Storming...
Never ending.
Always in his head.
He brought his hands up.
Over his ears.
Go away.
The voices drowned him.
Drenched him.
Loneliness his only friend.

*Again...*

> *And again...*

>> *And again...*

I'm not alone.

*The words were raw.*

*Empty.*

*But he knew them to be true.*

*If the voices stayed,*

*If they remained,*

*Then, he could never be alone.*

*He reached out his hand,*

*Into the loneliness.*

*And as it reached back, he pulled it forward.*

*Grappling,*

*Embracing,*

*And then...a blink.*

# TWENTY-THREE

Tomás opened his eyes, blinking away the crust from his eyelashes. It was like he was in a memory, waking again in that sterile, white infirmary after he'd conducted his first release. Except this time, no one waited at his bedside.

He slowly pushed himself up from the bed. No voices haunted him. All he could hear was the candle flickering in its perch on the wall.

After blinking a few more times, he peered around the room at the rows of beds.

His stomach dropped.

The bodies of his peers lay in the beds. Lifeless.

"Cevin?" he called out, voice hoarse. No one moved.

His joints ached as he climbed from the bed. The ground felt like he had just stepped off a ship, and he swayed to the side, nearly tripping over his long sleeping gown.

Once the room stopped spinning, he took his first step, glancing down at each of his peers. They slept with no signs of waking, a yellow-tinged smoke pooling from their orifices. His heart twisted with every sight.

Only to snap when he found Cevin sleeping in the same state as everyone else.

"Cevin!" Tomás raced to the bed, kneeling at Cevin's side and taking his stiff hand. "Come along now, Cevin— wake up. It is time to wake up...please."

Cevin remained still, his pale skin like paper, and his dusty blonde hair cascading over his face like rays of sunlight.

"Please..." Tomás begged, catching a tear in his throat. Why hadn't anyone else awoken? He counted the beds multiple times; each time, the number was the same. Fifteen still slept.

For how long?

He pressed his forehead to Cevin's hand, holding it there for what felt like hours. Tomás couldn't bring himself to look at Cevin's otherwise lifeless face. While he breathed, his crooked mouth opening and closing, each breath labored, pushing smoke into the air.

Only when the large wooden door to the infirmary opened did Tomás finally move.

Aelia entered the room, striding forward with the Mist on her heels. At first, she didn't notice Tomás, too busy checking each of the disciples, her lips pursed in a permanent frown. Tomás rose to his feet, his hands shaking as Aelia navigated around the beds.

Then she locked eyes with him. "You have awoken?"

"Senhora," Tomás bowed his head slightly, "I apologize that I did not stay in bed—I was confused upon waking and—"

She interjected, "It is fine. Come. Ningursu must know at once."

Aelia led Tomás to Ningursu's private study, tearing him away from Cevin's side. She did not say a word as they ascended the stairs. Nor did Tomás ask for an explanation.

With the other disciples lying in the infirmary, the Phrontistery pulsed with silence. While it had never been busy, the constant chatter echoed through the walls, while the voices never relented, always a hum in Tomás's head.

But now, there was nothing.

Not even Teodozia's voice, begging.

Aelia did not knock on Ningursu's door, tapping the knob once and sending the doors flying open. Ningursu sat at his desk, where a small basin of silver liquid glistened before him. He ran his finger over it, his thick brow furrowed, forming a crease on his forehead.

"Master Ningursu," Aelia said as she entered.

He raised his head. "Hello, Aelia...and Tomás."

"Senhor," Tomás lowered his head.

"Is he the only one then?" Ningursu asked Aelia.

"Yes, Master. I found him just now."

"Fascinating..." Ningursu rose, his silver eyes narrowing as he approached Tomás. "Why you, of all of them?"

Tomás did not reply, keeping his head low.

"Do not fret, Tomás. We are happy to have you here. It is just remarkable that you are the only one to join us. We thought everyone suffered the same fate as Teodozia."

Tomás swallowed, then asked, "But Teodozia went mad...didn't she? Everyone else is just...asleep."

"Ah, that is all because of Aelia," Ningursu said. "The potion that ended your life had an additional layer to it. If, upon escaping the darkness of death, the Mist proved too powerful, the potion was supposed to lock you in a deep slumber. Your peers remain in that slumber."

"But I did not," Tomás stated.

"You did not...and you are of sound mind, so it seems. And it did not take long either—merely a couple of days. Honestly, quite impressive."

"But what about…the others?" Tomás chose his words with care.

"All we can do is wait and see—and continue as we must."

"And what shall I do then, senhor?"

"You shall have the honor of continuing our sacred duty."

"Of releasing souls?"

"As I know you have been training to do," Ningursu said.

"Senhor?"

"Go—we shall reconvene when the time is right. I look forward to seeing your progress."

Before Tomás could ask any more questions, Aelia ushered him from the room, locking the door as he stumbled into the hallway alone.

# TWENTY-FOUR

Tomás changed out of his gown, pulling on his tunic and trousers and covering himself in the hooded cloak that Varden had given him. Before leaving, he took one of Cevin's many notes and folded it in his pocket, wearing it close to his chest. As much as he wanted to stay in the infirmary, holding Cevin's hand, Ningursu always watched. He had a duty—and for now, he'd abide by it.

While he had transitioned into the true role of a Mist Keeper, really his routine hadn't changed. He navigated through the Mist, listening for the last thoughts of others and releasing their souls. The only difference came when interacting with the living; naturally, he melded into the Mist, as undetectable as a ghost. But, when entering small villages, seeking food or shelter, he could push himself forward so those still alive could interact with him like anyone else.

Otherwise, it was all the same.

He released souls.

He traversed the Mist.

And eventually returned to the Phrontistery. Alone.

Ningursu and Aelia rarely graced him with their presence. His only company came from Cevin's lifeless body, his labored breaths an empty form of conversation. Even the ghosts loitering in the fortress provided little comfort.

Tomás had never really paid much attention to ghosts. They blended into their surroundings, faceless—or so they seemed.

Without Cevin distracting him, Tomás noticed their features more. They were still human at their core. Young, old, tall, short—human.

One ghost often loitered in the infirmary. At first, Tomás thought he was nothing more of him. But, in a certain light, the ghost reminded him of Ningursu. With wiry black hair and contemplative light eyes, the similarities were striking. But even if Tomás tried to listen to the ghost's thoughts, the Mist created a mask over the entire Phrontistery, leaving the voices silent.

Tomás never approached the ghost. Rather, in the evening, he returned to his bunk alone. Cevin's piles of unsent letters to his sister haunted the room. He didn't dare touch them, but every night, he stood over the pile, staring at Cevin's handwriting at the top of each letter.

*Dearest Edith.*

What would Edith do if Cevin never wrote again? How might Tomás tell her what became of her brother?

No. Cevin would wake again.

They made a promise to each other.

He just had to wait.


Moons passed. All remained constant.

The other disciples slept.

Ningursu and Aelia kept their secrets.

And Tomás released souls.

He rode the Mist far and wide but always returned to the Phrontistery, hoping that something would change.

Anything.

But nothing did.

Until one day, he arrived back at the Phrontistery to find Ningursu and Aelia waiting for him outside the infirmary.

"Good evening, Senhor, Senhora." Tomás lowered his head.

"Do not worry yourself with formalities, Tomás. We are here as your equals," Ningursu said.

"Equals?"

"You are a Mist Keeper and have done well in your current role. But there are more pressing matters. So please, come along. There is much to discuss."

Tomás glanced back at the infirmary doors. He had no choice but to follow, the Mist pulling at his ankles to keep pace with Ningursu and Aelia.

They led him up the stairs of the tower, as usual, without a word. Tomás tugged at the edge of his cloak, rubbing the material through his fingers as they ascended. With each step, the stairwell narrowed, bringing them to the top of the tower.

Aelia waved her hand just slightly, and the stairwell opened to the hidden room that Tomás found many moons earlier. He couldn't even be sure how long ago he had first ventured up these stairs—time had become such a blur in the passing days. Had he been a Mist Keeper in full for a month? A year? A decade?

He didn't know.

"I know you have been here before, Tomás," Ningursu said as he stepped into the hidden room. Yellow smoke rose around him, but unlike when Tomás entered the room alone, the smoke maintained a respectable distance.

"I am sorry, Senhor. The voices led me here," Tomás winced as he passed through the smoke. It pricked at his skin.

"There was no harm in your exploration. But now, we must provide you with an explanation," Ningursu waved another plume of smoke away, revealing two figures hunched over on the far wall.

Tomás's stomach churned. He recognized the first one; with wiry brown hair and its head falling to one side, it was hard to forget the creature that took Teodozia's voice. Every breath produced a raspy gasp, and as she lifted her head, her silver eyes darted in opposite directions.

The figure beside Teodozia was younger. In some respects, this one looked more human, but for the graying skin and balding scalp. Tomás squinted, then stepped back as the figure locked eyes with him.

"Elva?" he asked.

The creature extended its neck, but no voice responded.

"You are correct, Tomás. These creatures are what remains of Teodozia and Elva."

"But...what happened to them?"

Ningursu sighed, "The Mist is powerful...and often, it leads to madness. I spent thousands of years training disciples, but they each failed, succumbing to the Mist. That is...until Aelia." Ningursu nodded as the woman removed a vial of liquid from the cabinet on the wall. "When each Mist Keeper failed, they entered the Mist for good. But Aelia's magic allows her to understand the inner workings of the body, and she discovered that failure did not have to mean death. With the right combination of elements, she could prevent the Mist Keepers from fading...and harness their magic for the greater good."

"But...they aren't themselves, are they?" Tomás continued to stare at Teodozia and Elva.

Aelia spoke from her spot, "They died when they failed to ascend through the Mist. We are merely using what remains."

"But...I heard Teodozia."

"Echoes."

"Teodozia and Elva are gone," Ningursu reiterated. "Now, what remains can be used to defend against Tehuti Kek and the growing coalition of immortals. We can restore balance and pacify the oncoming storm."

Tomás frowned. They kept talking about a storm—about a war—but in his travels, he hadn't seen any signs of trouble. Cevin had witnessed it, supposedly, but where? Why was there so much talk but so little evidence?

Ningursu continued, "We tell you this, Tomás, because, unfortunately, it does not seem like the others will be recovering."

Tomás turned to Ningursu, locking eyes with him.

"We know you have been close with Cevin and the others, but...the Mist has not quelled for them. There is a storm inside their souls, and all we can do, I think, is honor them," Ningursu said.

"Honor them..." Tomás repeated.

"Yes. By using what remains, we can honor their magic and bring balance to the Mist. It is what each of you trained for...and what each of you wanted."

"I see," Tomás turned back to Teodozia. While her thoughts remained masked by the Mist, he could still recall the distant pleas for help. Was this what she wanted?

If she did...then why was she scared?

"As a Mist Keeper, you will stand beside us. It is your duty, after all, to the Mist," Ningursu said.

Tomás did not have another option. He bowed his head, and with his voice low, he recited, "I will do what is right for the Mist."

# TWENTY-FIVE

As soon as he returned to his bunk, Tomás collapsed on his bed, shaking. They were going to turn Cevin into a monster! What could he do to stop it? As much as he pleaded, Cevin never woke, locked in a purgatory between Life and Death.

He had heard Teodozia's pleas. While Ningursu had done well to mask her voice with the Mist, Tomás had still heard it many moons earlier. Would Cevin scream for help just like that? Would it be like when he sensed Teodozia's own collapse?

What could he do? He couldn't just walk away from Ningursu and Aelia. This was the only home he knew. There was no one waiting for him back in El Limra. And then there was Varden, who disappeared out to sea. Where could he find such a friendship again?

He paced his bunkroom, stealing glances at Cevin's letters. His sister wouldn't even know what became of him.

With a trembling hand, Tomás finally removed one of the letters from the end table. He unfolded it, reciting the words to himself.

*Dearest Edith,*
*I spent the last few weeks training with Ningursu—and I am scared.*

That letter ended with no further clarification. Tomás picked another off the table.

*Dearest Edith,*
*I worry that Tom and I might not survive this.*

And another.

*Dearest Edith,*
*I wonder what you would do in this predicament. I am witnessing war firsthand, but I do not understand its purpose.*

And one more.

*Dearest Edith,*
*If you are reading this, I am dead.*

"He planned out every letter...but never finished them..." Tomás whispered to himself, flipping through the pages. None of these letters would ever reach Edith. Unless...

He looked through the words. Could he use them to formulate a message and to let Edith know that her brother was gone?

It was the least he could do—in a way, Edith was his family...even if she never knew him.

With precision, he tore the papers, reconstructing the words on a blank page with a sticky adhesive that Cevin kept in one of his drawers. While the letter was not elegant, it told a simple story...and he hoped it would provide solace to Edith when she read it.

*Dearest Edith.*
*I am scared. I worry I will not survive this.*
*What would you do in this predicament?*
*I spent weeks training with Ningursu, but I think I am dead.*
*I hope you understand.*

*Your brother,*
*Cevin.*

The letter was disjointed, but it used Cevin's words. He would want this note to go to his sister, wouldn't he?

Tomás folded the letter. Then, with it close to his chest, he carried it out into the empty hallway. No one loitered, not even ghosts.

He moved through the fortress, climbing the stairwell back to the infirmary. Everyone still slept, undisturbed.

Tomás walked straight toward Cevin, sleeping there, frail and empty. Death had locked him in a time capsule. No stubble grew on his face, and his hair remained the same dusty blond. Only his skin had paled further, so pale he might have been a ghost.

"I know you're still there, Cev—I will not give up on you," he took Cevin's hand and squeezed it. "We made a promise."

He brought Cevin's cold hand to his lips and kissed it, holding it there, begging for any movement.

But the hand fell cold to the side, unchanged.

"I have written to your sister, so she knows what became of you. But I know one day, you'll be able to tell her yourself." Tomás rose, glancing again around the room. A single ghost stood by the doors, watching Tomás from afar.

"I'll be right back, Cev. I promise," Tomás whispered and turned toward the ghost. As he approached, the ghost's features—so similar to Ningursu, yet with a less defined nose and chin—came into focus.

Tomás inhaled once, then extended the letter. "Are you able to deliver this to Cevin's sister?"

The ghost glanced at the folded paper. Then, with an ever-so-subtle nod, he pocketed it.

"Thank you, senhor," Tomás said.

The ghost did not reply, turning away from Tomás and phasing into the Mist.

# TWENTY-SIX

At first, nothing changed about Tomás's daily routine. He completed his releases, then returned to the Phrontistery...alone.

But it wasn't long before Aelia and Ningursu made their presence known, visiting the infirmary daily and bringing a collection of different potions and elixirs to the disciples. Tomás watched from afar as Aelia opened each disciple's mouth, pouring different liquids down their throats. A few of them wreathed, showing the first signs of life in ages, before succumbing once again to their sleep. When she reached Cevin, Tomás looked away, not able to watch as Cevin twitched and exhaled a single plume of yellow smoke.

Ningursu said they wanted to do this right—to ensure that the Mist Keepers would be honored. But what was so honorable about this torture?

Yet, Tomás could do nothing but watch. He had no way of saving Cevin and the others.

He just had to obey.

A forever obedient servant.

Pacified by the Mist.

Some days, he considered walking away from it all. But to leave Cevin? To leave everyone? It was beyond his abilities. He had no place to go...and no skills beyond what he had learned at the Phrontistery.

So, everything remained.

Constant.

Unchanging.

Except for the bodies of his peers, twitching and wreathing beneath the power of Aelia's strange elixirs.

So, it was hard to miss when a newcomer arrived on the horizon, walking across the Schanifeld toward the Phrontistery. Tomás saw them as they approached in the distance, a mere speck on the horizon one day as he finished his releases. He paused, watching as they approached. It could have been any common person wandering along the fields.

But, as the figure drew closer, their thoughts broke through the smoke, clear and determined.

*It's right there, isn't it? Just as he said.*

Why would a newcomer visit the Phrontistery? Mostly, only the Mist Keepers took notice of the fortress. Occasionally, a visitor might wander up from town, but it was only to deliver goods and services.

As long as Tomás had been here, the Phrontistery had been impenetrable.

But the figure kept walking straight toward him. Tomás froze, unable to take his eyes off the figure. Should he warn Ningursu? Aelia? But what would he say? He didn't even know if this person was a threat!

But could they be that immortal, Tehuti Kek, coming to end the Mist Keepers for good? To destroy balance?

He took a step forward, trying to delve more into the invader's mind.

*I'm coming, Cevin.*

Tomás's lip twitched. His letter must have made it to Edith! Was she coming now to be by Cevin's side in the final hours?

It had to be her—who else would be coming?

Tomás resisted the urge to burst into a run, taking each step with care as he approached the figure in the distance.

There, she appeared from the smoke, her red hair billowing in the wind behind her. On her hip, she wore a sword layered with chain mail armor that made her body look all the smaller. With the freckles on her round face and the sparkle in her eyes, there was no denying that she was Cevin's sister.

Tomás raised his hand as he approached her.

Before he could speak, she unsheathed her sword.

Her thoughts did not give away her next move.

In one motion, she launched toward Tomás and pinned him to the ground, holding the sword to his jugular.

"Where is he, Reaper?" she hissed. Unlike Cevin, her voice slithered through the air like a snake weaving through the grass.

"R-reaper?" Tomás stammered.

"You might call yourselves Mist Keepers, but I know what you really are. Reaping everything this world has to offer. So, tell me...where is he?"

"You mean...you mean Cevin?"

"Who else?" Edith asked.

"I'll show you. I'm Tomás, his...his bunkmate. I...I can show you."

"I do not need your help. Just tell me where he is." She dug the blade deeper into his neck.

Tomás choked.

"Now!"

"In the Phrontistery...in the infirmary. He's...he's gone."

"Liar!"

"He hasn't woken in ages. They're honoring him."

"And what does that mean?" Edith snarled..

"They intend to use his magic to protect the Mist—to keep the balance."

Edith laughed, "Cevin would never have agreed to that."

"I know..." Tomás mumbled.

"You know?"

"I told you—I was his bunkmate. We were...close. I know he wouldn't have wanted that."

"You say that...but here you are, not stopping them?" Edith cocked her head to the side. "That doesn't make you any better, does it, Reaper?"

"I cannot stop them. I am but their obedient servant."

"No. You are complacent. And that is just as bad."

"I—"

Edith removed the sword from Tomás's throat. From the corner of his eye, it almost seemed like the blade had shrunken into a sharp dagger. But he didn't have the chance to process the image.

Edith took a step back, glowering down at Tomás. As he sat up from the ground, she smirked.

Then lunged at him.

He didn't even have time to react as Edith sliced his face, the blade undoing his skin like a meal at the dinner table. Tomás gasped out and toppled back to the ground. His right eye twitched as if a thousand grains of sand had entered his socket.

"Please, stop!" he cried out, blood oozing into his mouth.

Edith laughed, extending her blade again, this time so it hit him in the stomach. He screamed as she removed the blade. His breaths could not complete a single gasp, hanging loose on each raspy note.

"I think that will do, Reaper. Consider yourself spared...for now."

"Wait," Tomás begged.

But Edith just laughed, wiping her blade clean as she walked through the flowers of the Schanifeld, painting the white petals red with Tomás's blood.

# TWENTY-SEVEN

Tomás crawled through the flowers. With each drop of blood, the flowers wilted around him, forming a collection of black splatters on the otherwise white field. One benefit of being dead was that he could not die again, but the pain remained, clawing at him, threatening to put him into an endless slumber.

With every movement, spots danced over his vision. His head lulled to the side. Ningursu and Aelia would find him, right? If he just closed his eyes for a little while...surely, they would find him.

He pressed his face into the dirt. *Cevin*, he thought to himself. *Your sister is coming, Cevin.*

His vision grew spotty.

And alone, he could only turn to the voices, reciting phrases in the distance, humming the solemn tune of death.

*Help me.*

*I'm sorry.*

*Mama!*

*Goodbye.*

*Oh!*

*Tom?*

*It'll be okay now.*

*Tom!?*

*Time to rest.*

*Tom!*

"Tomás, stay with me...you'll be okay," someone said.

Tomás's head rocked to the side as he opened his eyes. He rested in someone's arms, carrying him above the ground.

"Stay with me," they said again, their voice familiar.

He squinted through his fuzzy vision at his rescuer: tall, with kempt red hair and a long face. Even after years, he still recognized his rescuer.

"Vardy?" he moaned.

"Rest. You will heal soon. Just stay with me, Tomás."

"What—how—"

"I will explain when all is well—just focus on me."

Tomás nodded slightly, resting his head against Varden's chest, flickering in and out of consciousness.

Before finding himself again in a dream.

# TWENTY-EIGHT

Dreams bobbed like waves against the surface. In and out, they rocked Tomás in his sleep. Somewhere, deep in his core, he knew they were dreams, horrible dreams, about blood, yellow smoke, and screams.

But he couldn't wake.

Instead, he slept, surrounded by the commotion.

Begging...

Pleading...

Until finally, a jolt pulled him awake.

There, he found himself in a small room with a single porthole window letting in daylight. Once again, he was back on the ship, traveling far away from El Limra, toward the unknown.

Had it all been a dream?

He squinted. A bandage obstructed half of his vision. As he sat up, pain rippled through his abdomen.

"Ack!" he cursed to himself, collapsing back on the cot.

The door swung open at once. Varden ducked into the room, his head nearly hitting the beam of the doorframe. "Tomás! You have awoken."

Tomás stared at Varden with his unhindered eye. Varden looked almost exactly how he remembered. Slightly older now but still with his slick red hair and kind maroon eyes. It was like a memory had crawled out of Tomás's own mind, standing right there before him.

"How did I end up here?" Tomás asked.

"Do you not remember?" Varden sat in the chair next to Tomás's cot.

"I..." Tomás wracked his brain before recalling, "Edith."

Varden nodded, letting Tomás continue.

"She had come to rescue her brother...but she attacked me. I tried to talk to her..." Tomás locked his eye with Varden. "Then...then I tried to crawl back to the Phrontistery...but...I suppose I failed to reach it..."

Varden brought his hands together and pressed them to his chin. "Good...so you do remember at least."

"I am perplexed though as to what happened. Her thoughts were jumbled—" Tomás stopped himself from continuing. What would Varden think if Tomás confessed to reading thoughts?

But Varden did not seem phased. "I fear things are more complicated than you are aware, Tomás." While he punctuated the statement, Varden's thoughts continued. *Ningursu's lies may be difficult for you to see.*

Tomás inhaled once, then said, "Well, as of this moment, I am baffled by what occurred with Edith yesterday."

"It was a week ago. You lost a lot of blood and needed time to recover."

"Oh," he turned his head toward the porthole. Through its musty glass, the waves of the sea bounced against the ship, not a single slither of land in sight. His heart skipped. What happened to Cevin and the other disciples? Did Edith save them?

And what of Ningursu and Aelia? Did they even know he had disappeared?

Why did Varden save him...and not them?

His throat twisted, and he gripped the woolen blanket close. A single tear fell down his cheek.

Varden placed a hand on his shoulder. "Let me get you something to eat and drink, then I'll help you understand what happened. I am so sorry, Tomás... I had hoped we would not meet again like this."

Tomás did not reply to Varden, pulling the blanket closer and shutting his eye once again.

But this time, the dreams did not return.

Varden sat with Tomás as he picked at his plate of beans. Tomás didn't speak, pushing the legumes around the plate, hardly eating. Memories flooded over him, masking even the distant chattering of voices. Every time he closed his eyes, he saw Edith pinning him to the ground, a blade morphing in size within her grasp.

He touched the bandage on his face. Finally, he found the courage to ask, "Is it gone?"

"Is what gone?" Varden replied.

"My eye."

"It is damaged beyond repair. I am sorry."

"Oh...oh." Tomás placed the plate of beans on the ground and picked up his lukewarm cup of tea. His hands shook as he brought it to his lips.

Varden frowned. "If I had known Edith was on a rampage, I would have stopped her. She seemed quite calm when we arrived in port."

"You are acquainted with Edith?"

Varden nodded. "She had been traveling with us for a couple of years now...soon after I left you with the Phrontistery."

"But then...how did Cev—her brother write to her? You were at sea."

"Nedo helped."

"Nedo?"

"The ghost who delivered that letter you constructed."

"You know I constructed it?"

Varden smiled, "I know plenty."

Tomás pocketed that comment for later, letting his mouth fall closed.

"When Nedo delivered that letter to us, Edith begged the captain to divert at once. It was clear that something was amiss, especially since she hadn't heard from her brother in months. While I was never that close to her, I could tell that the letter had affected her. She spent her days mulling about the ship, muttering and sharpening her metals. I don't think she even slept.

"Once we arrived in port, she jumped from the ship before we even finished docking. She had not told a soul of her plans. All I can infer is that when she saw you, a Mist Keeper, her anger and frustration came to a front...so she attacked."

"But...Cevin always spoke fondly of his sister. I cannot imagine him being fond of—" Tomás chose his words, "someone so...volatile."

"My understanding is that Edith was always very protective of her brother...and even more concerned about his studies at the Phrontistery. She ranted endlessly about his letters and how they had grown more scattered...and more scared. There were multiple times when she was determined to go rescue him."

Tomás wrung his hands together and crossed his legs. He had read Cevin's letters. After Teodozia's failed transition, his notes to Edith had been filled with pain. Such a happy young man worn down by endless studies.

Edith must have sensed the same thing.

"It did not help that we had spent quite a few months in Merton either," Varden continued. "Kek has their own opinions on the Phrontistery and the Mist Keepers...and I believe Edith took those opinions to heart."

Tomás stared at Varden. "Kek? You mean...Tehuti Kek? The immortal?"

Varden nodded.

"You...are affiliated with the Palaver of Immortals?" Tomás scooted back from Varden ever so slightly.

"Yes and no."

"What are you saying?"

"We are affiliated, but we do not take part in their wars and affairs."

Tomás stared at Varden, his mind churning. Everything had come to him in pieces, and now when he tried to put them together, the adhesive to hold them together just would not stick.

Varden rose, running his hand along one of the beams, and continued. "For many years, Captain Huo acted on a treaty of neutrality. We served both Tehuti Kek and the Phrontistery as a chartered ship to conduct business—delivering people and products where needed. We were perfectly content in this arrangement...but our neutrality ultimately ended. I believe it was around the time we delivered you to the Phrontistery, actually. A few months prior, Kek had offered our captain a taste of immortality, but not without a cost. The deal was to stop serving the Mist Keepers and become the Palaver of Immortal's chartered vessel. It was a tempting offer...and ultimately, our captain obliged."

Tomás kept watching Varden. "So does that mean your captain is an immortal?"

"Yes."

"And...what about you?"

Varden grimaced, choosing his words as he spoke, "I did have a taste about a year ago."

Tomás took a step back from Varden.

*Trust me, Tomás. We are not here to harm you,* Varden's voice rang, before he spoke aloud, "What makes your current life state so different from mine?"

"I—" Tomás opened his mouth, then shook his head. Varden had a point.

So instead, he diverted to a different question. "Why would an immortal care about a chartered ship?"

"Why would a Mist Keeper?"

"Well, um—"

Varden chuckled, cutting Tomás off. "It is not the ship but who is on it. Kek's interest lies in the magic on board. The people. They see us as potential warriors in their army."

"But you said you are not involved in their battles."

"We're not...but it does not stop Kek from trying to woo us."

Tomás continued to search Varden's mind. No thoughts warned of deception. Varden, standing there with his head hitting the ceiling and red eyes scanning Tomás, was the same as years prior, trustworthy and kind.

But the truth left Tomás with a pang in his head and an ache in his heart.

Now, he just wanted to be alone, to process the pains and sort through the truths.

# TWENTY-NINE

Tomás kept to himself for the following days, re-familiarizing himself with the ship and ignoring the constant barrage of voices. He kept his attention focused on the sea and his heart resting on Cevin. His mind wandered to everything Varden told him. Here he was, aboard an enemy ship. While he trusted Varden, the others left him wondering.

Voices repeated.

*Where are we taking this Reaper?*

*He doesn't seem menacing.*

*Least he could do is help out.*

Tomás let the voices sink into his chest. It was a good point: where were they going? What happened to Edith? Was the crew trustworthy?

After a few days, he finally gathered himself and approached Varden in the galley.

"Hello, Tomás," Varden said without turning.

"How did you know it was me?"

"I always know," Varden faced him. "What are you thinking?"

"I wanted more answers..." Tomás tugged at the edge of his shirt cuff, where a small piece of his old cloak remained hidden.

"And I will provide them to you."

Tomás paused, then asked, "Where are we going?"

"Away," Varden's lip curved slightly. "I do not know our exact destination, but Captain Huo was determined to get as far away from the Schanifeld and Merton as possible."

"Why?"

"With Edith attacking you, even if she is not truly affiliated with Kek, it has brought the battle to a new level. As I mentioned, we have no intentions in participating...so after I found you, we fled."

Tomás scowled. He didn't dare mention the monsters that Aelia and Ningursu had created.

Even the thought made his heart sink, with Cevin's name echoing with each fallen thump.

"What other questions do you have?" Varden asked.

Tomás pondered, then asked, "Why did you bring me aboard? If I am a Mist Keeper, then wouldn't I be at risk of bringing the war to your ship?"

"I know you, Tomás. At your core, you are a pacifist trying to do what is right. While some might change their belief systems so easily, yours is a part of your core nature."

"We only were acquainted for a few weeks...and I was clueless then. How could you be so sure?"

"Because I know things quite well."

"I do not follow."

Varden chuckled, a deep rumbling noise that rocked his body. "I told you how Kek's interest lies not in the ship but in the crew. That's because of our magic."

"Magic...right."

"Each member of this crew has a magical talent. Some are stronger than others. For instance, Edith manipulates metal."

"That explains the knives," Tomás commented.

"Yes, her knives," Varden shook his head. "There is so much more that she could do with that type of metallurgy, but she chose knives."

"It is a weapon."

"Yes, but magic is also a path for creativity. There are those who can create artistry out of plants or sculpt from the lava in the earth. Or there is our own captain, who can manipulate water and form creatures from its very surface."

"That sounds...fascinating," Tomás said. Yet, the mere thought left his stomach churning. This was the magic that Ningursu and Aelia had been warning them about in class. It was the type that broke the balance and threatened the very sanctity of Life and Death.

Right?

He glanced back at Varden, "And what about you?"

"Oh...I have intuition," Varden replied with a smile.

"Intuition?"

Varden's red eyes glistened. "That is what I call it. Some people call us seers, others call us Medii...but I like to call it intuition. I can see the dead, I can understand the truths about the living, and sometimes—on rare occasions—I can see the future."

"The future?"

"Exactly. How do you think I knew we would meet again?"

"I thought you were just being nice."

"No, it was blurry, but I saw you back on board this ship with me. Under what circumstances? I did not know until they occurred." Varden leaned against one of the barrels. "Some seers see more clearly, some not at all. It just depends on our talents."

"So, you couldn't stop Edith from doing...this," Tomás reached to his bandaged eye.

"Unfortunately, that is beyond my abilities. Which is why Kek has less interest in me compared to other seers. It's why I left with the captain a few years ago. Kek had acquired me as a potential seer, but since my talents didn't match their expectations, they let me go."

A whole slew of questions wrapped around Tomás. Despite Varden being a constant in the back of his mind, he didn't truly know the man. Where did he come from? What talents lay hidden beneath his fingertips?

And Varden, with his intuition, seemed to know Tomás's thoughts. "We have time to learn more about each other, Tomás. The ship will be at sea for many days."

Tomás's lip twitched, "I thought I was the one who read thoughts."

"You read thoughts?"

Tomás managed a very slight laugh. It was his turn to answer questions.

# THIRTY

They continued to sail across the sea, with no signs of land for many weeks. In that time, Varden and Tomás talked. There was something comforting about Varden. His thoughts held no signs of deception. And every word he spoke bore honesty like no other.

As the ship traveled further south, Tomás told Varden of his time at the Phrontistery. While he never highlighted every aspect of his teachings, he spoke of his time learning to become a Mist Keeper and harnessing his abilities. He glossed over his time with Cevin, though; it felt weird mentioning Cevin to Varden. It wasn't as though Tomás had a relationship with the giant, but...the mere subject caused his heart to twist.

There were times when Tomás could not shake Varden from his thoughts. He admired man's delicate nature, his artfully combed hair, and the low rumble of his laugh. As Varden deconstructed his own past, Tomás spent his evenings recanting it, placing those stories into a chest in the back of his mind.

Varden told Tomás how Kek recruited him as a young boy from the far-off nation of Delilah. One of the few giants with magic, he caught Kek's attention in their travels. There, he left home, to the disappointment of his parents, to work alongside Kek as their personal seer.

Yet, in contrast to his predecessors, Varden claimed his magic did not reach the same strengths. His visions often met uncertainty, and he was less than enthusiastic about chatting with the dead. In his words, he enjoyed the heightened sense of understanding people and delving into their overall being. For Kek, this was not useful, and when Captain Huo came, they had no reason to stop Varden from leaving. Already they had acquired another seer, an astute young man named Yeshua, who managed to predict each of the Mist Keeper's attacks without fault.

Varden had been on board the ship for nearly ten years. In that time, he helped transport countless disciples to the Phrontistery. Not just Tomás.

And this included Cevin.

When Cevin's name crossed Varden's lips, Tomás froze.

"You met Cevin?" Tomás asked as they stared out at sea.

"Ah yes, he was a good kid. Talkative. Insightful. A little lost. But a good kid," Varden grinned. "I know you were close with him."

Tomás flushed.

"That is how Edith came to know us. She was desperate to join our crew when we plucked Cevin from his home. But we didn't have the space. Even then, she was...terrifying. Her magic was limited at the time, but that didn't stop her from threatening to cut off our fingers if we harmed Cevin. To quell her, one of our crew members—Nedo, the ghost—told her he would be the messenger between her and her brother. It seemed to quell her until a few years later when she finally joined our ship."

Tomás nodded, watching as another wave thrashed against the ship. Everything was entwined, from magic and mist to life and death.

"I do hope Nedo is okay," Varden remarked. "He stayed behind at the Phrontistery."

"He is a ghost...what might harm him?"

Varden frowned. "To be honest, I am not sure...but he was always fearful of the Mist Keepers. You're a young one...but I am sure the older ones have power we cannot even fathom."

"Right." Tomás wrung his hands together, tracing the horizon with his single good eye. In the distance, storm clouds bobbed with the waves. With the sun reflecting on them, they almost looked yellow.

The days continued. Tomás spent most of his day sharing stories with Varden, assisting on board where possible, and turning his attention toward the sea, holding close to a single word: *Cevin*.

There, he would watch the waves. Some days, Captain Huo would perform feats of magic, sculpting sea serpents and sirens out of the sea, telling stories, and laughing with the other crewmates. Tomás never partook in the events, keeping to himself and watching the crew. Varden often stood to the side, that usual smirk on his lips. When their eyes locked, Tomás turned away, bringing himself back to reality with his constant, with Cevin. There just wasn't space in his heart for Varden. Not when Cevin's future remained as murky as the barrels of mead on board the ship.

Once they made landfall, he had to find a way back to Cevin.

Or...whatever remained of him.

The mere thought of the monstrosities that Ningursu and Aelia were creating left his throat dry. He hadn't brought them up to Varden yet. How could he describe what Ningursu and Aelia were creating? He hadn't even seen the final product.

Only one thing he knew for certain: these creatures left his body writhing, trapped in a nightmare.

But...he couldn't imagine Cevin carrying that sort of weight.

So, he kept those concerns close to his chest, even as the shoreline came into view.

It happened the same day Varden finally removed the bandage from his eye. Tomás sat on his bed, and with delicate hands, Varden unwound the bandage. As the last bit of adhesive tore from his skin, Tomás winced.

"You could look worse," Varden said and handed Tomás a small mirror.

Tomás peered at his reflection. A jagged scar cut through his face from the corner of his right eyebrow, slicing at his eyelid before crossing his nose and resting on his lip. Behind the scar, a white cataract had fallen over his eye, leaving behind a cloud of white in his vision.

A permanent reminder of what had befallen him.

*Really, not bad at all.* Varden's voice echoed.

Tomás traced the scar. "I suppose it shows that I survived my first battle."

"Hopefully, it is your only battle."

"Do you not see another?"

"None that are strong enough to enter my vision."

They sat there for a moment in silence, only for it to be interrupted by the clanking of a bell.

Varden sat up at once, "That means we have found land."

"Really? Where are we then?"

"Not a clue—but the sea always takes us where needed. So, we're here now. Come on," Varden bounded from the room, ducking under the doorway on his way out.

Tomás glanced one last time at his reflection. The man in the mirror stared back, tired and lost, with no control over his future.

# THIRTY-ONE

L and approached, a mere shadow against a dense cloud of smoke. Tomás joined Varden on deck, squinting with his good eye.

"This is not normal sea fog," Varden whispered.

Tomás agreed with a nod. The fog weighed on his shoulders while voices hummed in his ear. This fog was alive, in a way, watching every movement, counting every second. This was the Mist laying its claim.

They stood in silence as the shadow of the land neared. No one spoke. Even their thoughts grew quiet.

The port that greeted them bore the same silence. No merchants loitered with their wares. The ships sharing dock appeared to be permanent fixtures, their sails untouched, and activity nothing but a hum.

"What occurred here?" Tomás asked.

Varden stared, his brow furrowed. "I...am not sure. But it occurred a long time ago, and this place has never recovered since."

"You've never been here?"

"No, I do not recognize it. But I am sure the captain knows this place."

Tomás frowned but said nothing. He focused instead past the port, towards the greenery suffocating against the fog. The vague outline of buildings watched over them from the hill.

Why didn't he feel more excited? While he had traversed the Mist across the Schanifeld, this was only the third place he'd traveled to without Death as his guide. He grew up in El Limra, lived his adolescence in the Phrontistery, and now...he was here.

But everything about this location felt...dead. Like he had never left the Schanifeld.

Perhaps that was part of being a Mist Keeper. The world lost its allure, replaced with the endless barrage of dead voices and souls begging for attention.

Even once the ship finished docking, there was no excitement to leave. Tomás merely stood there, watching as the crew disembarked, wobbling as they tried to regain their sea legs.

Varden once again joined Tomás's side, "We're in São Caméliosa."

"São Caméliosa? You mean the Capital of Gonvernnes?"

"That's right."

Tomás picked at his nails. He vaguely recalled soldiers selecting protégé at La Catedral, giving them an opportunity to show their magic and prowess. They would take them to São Caméliosa to train.

If he saw any of them, would they remember him now?

Then again, he didn't remember them either.

"Would you like to disembark?" Varden asked.

"I would, but...it looks quite miserable, doesn't it?" Tomás said.

"Oh, what is a bit of fog to a Mist Keeper like you?"

Tomás didn't reply.

"Please, would you join me? As a friend?" Varden requested, locking eyes with Tomás.

At once, Tomás turned away, Varden's red eyes causing his entire body to twist. Those eyes were like when the last bit of sunset, painting the sky deep mahogany and capturing the final sigh before sleep.

But as much as he itched to stare into them, there was another color that mattered more.

"Alright, I shall join you," Tomás whispered. But instead of turning back to Varden, he kept his eyes locked on the silver waves of the water.

They did not speak as they left port, walking up the hill to the quiet city. White flowers lined the paths of São Caméliosa, seeming to struggle against the constant beat of smoke. Their flowers curled for any bit of light, while the surrounding trees barely coughed the color green.

It took Tomás a bit to regain his land legs, catching himself on Varden's arm as he stumbled to the side. Varden smirked at him, but Tomás was quick to brush himself off and march a few steps forward to avoid making eye contact with the giant.

They had no destination in mind as they wandered through the city. It was different than the town near the Phrontistery or even El Limra. Despite the pull of smoke, vines and roots composed the buildings, woven together like a sculpture. Back in La Catedral, they prayed to L'Corona Verde, telling stories of her magical control of plants. Is this where she lived?

Was she waiting in the intricate castle at the top of the hill, guarded by a garden with evenly cut hedges?

Tomás gawked at it as he and Varden approached, squinting with his one good eye. A gate sat open, welcoming any visitors from the path.

"I sense...quite potent magic here," Varden whispered. "Or...there used to be."

"L'Corona Verde?" Tomás asked.

"Who?"

"Oh...it was the goddess that we prayed to in La Catedral...back in El Limra."

"Gods and goddesses are merely people who flaunt their power."

"I suppose," Tomás agreed.

"But...there was power here..." Varden took another step forward, reading the text on the sign. *la Propriedad d'los Gardeniros n'e Diversito.*

As Tomás read the text to himself, a slew of whispers entered his mind, overlapping with each other and turning his attention in circles.

He shook them away, focusing on Varden as he ducked underneath the arch. "Varden, are you sure we should go inside there?"

"Why not? It is open."

"But...if there is power inside..."

"Why are you concerned? You are already dead, Tomás."

He had a point, but Tomás didn't humor him.

Side-by-side, they continued inside the garden, weaving in and out of the vine-laden paths. Shrubbery, trees, and flowers swayed with the wind.

At first, Tomás did not notice the guards lining the path. But, as they continued forward, taking in the artistry of the trees, he saw them, camouflaged with roots layering their bodies like armor. They didn't flinch as he and Varden walked down the path, nor did they react as Varden picked one flower from a bush and held it to the sun.

As he stared at it, his pupils shrunk, like pinpoint. His red iris glowed with sunlight. As he stared forward, his mouth opened, hanging there, not a breath escaping his lips.

"Varden?" Tomás touched his friend's arm.

No response.

"Hello? Varden!?" He shook his friend.

The giant stumbled. The flower fell from his hand.

Then, like a tree, he fell to the ground.

# THIRTY-TWO

Tomás tugged Varden's body off the path, using a bundle of leaves as a pillow to rest his head. A few of the guards glanced down the path, but none of them left their spots, unmovable like the trees.

"Varden...c'mon...wake up," Tomás shook his friend's shoulder. "I fear I won't be able to carry you back to the ship. Please...wake up."

For a moment, he was back in the infirmary with Cevin, pleading for his constant to wake. He couldn't lose anyone else; he couldn't have another ripped from him by magic.

After a few moments, Varden stirred. His eyes opened abruptly, darting around the area before locking onto Tomás's face.

"Varden...are you alright?" Tomás asked.

"Yes...I believe so. Are you?"

"What do you mean?"

"You look...frightened."

"Well, you did just collapse."

"Yes...I did..." Varden sat up from the ground, shaking the leaves from his hair. "I apologize. I believe I had a...vision."

"As in you saw the future?"

"I am uncertain."

"Do you want to return to the ship?" Tomás asked.

"No...let us continue exploring. Perhaps I will better understand my vision then."

Tomás didn't argue with Varden, helping him from the ground. Together, in a shared silence, they continued along the path, admiring the trees and flowers while avoiding contact with the plant-covered guards. Varden seemed to walk in a haze as they navigated the paths.

In their shared silence, Tomás's attention turned to the distant hum of voices. There, they beckoned him, the task of the release tickling his fingers. Wasn't his job to still release souls? Despite being taken from the Phrontistery, did he not have a duty to perform?

They slowed their pace as they entered a sculpture garden at the edge of the stone castle. Unamused facades of royalty lined the path, with etchings of stories long past on their surface. Varden walked forward, his attention pointed at the statue in the center of the courtyard. With a flower crown and stoic features, the statue did not look distinct from the others...except for the crystalized white flower in her hands.

*I do not trust those two.* A voice whispered in Tomás's ear.

He glanced around as they approached but saw no one.

Varden reached for the crystalized flower. But, before his fingers touched the petals, dark thorns shot from the statue's palm, forming a cage around the flower.

"Leave L'Corona Verde's camellia be," someone called from the trees.

Tomás turned. While a few guards had emerged from the tree line, the voice did not belong to them.

Rather, a small figure with dark eyes and a wide forehead lowered from a nearby tree branch. The man crossed his arms, glowering up at both Tomás and Varden.

"We apologize," Tomás quickly said.

But Varden was quick to add, "That is L'Corona Verde?"

The small man nodded.

"That is not what she looks like," Varden whispered. "She's shorter...freckled...with a round face. When she smiles, her top teeth appear larger than her bottom row."

While she's small, she's powerful, with an arm composed of vines...and a flower nestled behind her ear. Even in her eyes...there's this kindness. She is not like...this."

"How would you know?"

"Because...I saw her in a vision...and she's going to save the world."

Tomás stared at Varden. The statement was objective, grounded in fact rather than opinion.

"What makes you say that?" Another guard asked.

Varden turned back to the statue, "I saw her in a vision of the future. She was smiling and laughing, wielding flowers on her fingertips. Because of her, finally, the balance of Life and Death will know peace. The world will chant her name... No, they'll sing it. They will say how she brought peace with laughter and beauty. She'll make the world green."

Tomás continued to stare at Varden. What he said came with no preliminary thoughts, as if this was an innate fact locked inside of him.

The small man smirked. "Ah, so you're a Medii."

Varden nodded, "A seer. Yes."

The guards murmured.

"Well, I did not expect to meet a seer again after everything that has happened...but I am happy to be proven wrong," the small man said.

"I was not deemed eligible," Varden remarked.

Tomás frowned, but Varden's thoughts provided no answers.

"That is good to hear. Many unnecessary lives have been lost," the man replied.

Varden nodded. "Yes, I know."

"But you are here, Senhor...?"

"Varden. And this is my friend, Tomás."

"I am Yusef," the man said. "Pleasure to meet you, Senhor Varden. I am wondering if you would do us the honor of detailing your vision so that we may record it? In the name of L'Corona Verde?"

"Of course." Varden glanced at Tomás. "You can come, too, if you'd like. Or...you can return to the ship."

Tomás fidgeted, then said, "I'd like to learn as well...so I'll come with you. If that is permissible."

Varden smiled, "It always is, Tom."


Yusef and a few other Gardeniros led Varden and Tomás to their barracks, where they gathered by an old, knotted table beneath dim candlelight. They removed a large scroll of paper inscribed with a slew of different handwriting. Each of them touched the scroll and then took their positions along the wall, except for Yusef and an older woman with a crown of flowers in her hair.

"Please, take a seat," Yusef said.

Tomás and Varden obeyed.

"This is our Abedesa, Senhora Xóchitl. She will record what you saw," Yusef pulled out a seat for the old woman. She smiled at him, then took a seat, picking the thin wooden pen from the table and dabbing it with ink. Varden stared at the parchment, his face unflinching as he scanned the page. "This is centuries of history, isn't it?"

"Of times past and future, all with the help of seers," Yusef said. "The Gardeniros have long not just been the protectors of La Propriedad, but also the history of this kingdom...especially after the Great Wilting. We have relied on seers to understand that event...and help us believe that the future might bloom one day."

"What is the Great Wilting?" Tomás asked.

"Ah, that is the very foundation of our history. Once, many centuries ago, São Caméliosa was the home of powerful magic that transcended the globe. We, the Gardeniros, wielded it, bringing greenery and spring to the world with a flick of our fingers. We composed forests, brought good harvests, and acted as the conduit for Life. It was a different time when things were met with balance.

"But, as the story goes, that all changed when a man cloaked in smoke arrived in the city. He took away each piece of magic with a single breath. With it, he left behind a mere corpse of what once was our home." Yusef shared a sad glance with Xóchitl, then continued. "While there have been many names for this man, many seers have confirmed one truth: he was nothing more but Death."

The blood rushed from Tomás's face. He pulled his feet onto the chair, gripping his ankles in trepidation. Could it really be who he thought? Surely, there must have been a reason for such a decision.

As if Varden knew Tomás's own questions, he asked, "Why would Death have a feud with those who wield Life?"

Xóchitl finally spoke, her voice like the wind, "That is one question our seers could never answer."

No one spoke for a moment. Tomás's head raced, stomping out the echoes of other voices. Ningursu and Aelia lectured about maintaining the balance of Life and Death. Surely, they couldn't be the same ones to leave São Caméliosa in a plume of smoke, right?

Besides, how would the seers really know?

How would the Gardeniros know now?

"What if none of it is true?" Tomás finally questioned.

Xóchitl stared at him, her green eyes unwavering as she analyzed his every movement. Her thoughts showed no sign of malice, and her voice remained calm with her answer, "The trees never forget...and their stories are always true. And right now, the trees are dying, and the earth has turned to dust. Even if there is no veracity to the stories, there is something amiss in our world. Do you not agree?"

Tomás crossed his legs, turning his attention away from the woman and back to the old parchment paper. There may have been something awry in the world...but it was all Tomás ever knew.

# THIRTY-THREE

For hours, Varden sat with the Gardeniros, detailing his vision of L'Corona Verde. Yet, as their discussions of magic grew, Tomás receded, eventually leaving the barracks and returning to the gardens. There was a shared understanding between Varden and the Gardeniros; they were all products of Life, their magic alive and powerful. Tomás, on the other hand, operated in a different world.

He belonged to the dead, to releasing their souls and to bringing them peace. But would there be peace as long as there was war? The Gardeniros waited for L'Corona Verde to bring peace...but how long might that take? How many years did Varden see into the future to find her, laughing and blossoming?

Would she ever return, especially after Death stole the magic of the Gardeniros? Unless that was but a story used to explain the otherwise unexplainable.

But with the weight of the dead on Tomás's shoulders, he wondered whether Death had returned since what they called the Great Withering. They cried out to him as he left the garden, a constant barrage, like a bell or a drum.

*Good night.*

*Father?*

*I'm sorry.*

*Goodbye love.*

He inhaled once, reaching into his cuff where the piece of tattered fabric remained. With it as his protector, he found himself at the edge of the forest. The trees twisted with vines and roots. As he stared at each one, he noted their differences, each one telling a different story.

Beneath their roots, those final thoughts continued to echo.

He brushed his hand over the tree. Each one represented a single soul waiting for a chance for freedom. How long had they been waiting?

Well, that didn't matter. Tomás knew what had to be done.

At least he had one purpose.

Tomás released souls until the sun set, then wandered back to the ship, unseen as the Mist cloaked him. He had lost count of how many souls clamored for his touch. Nor did he know how many remained.

He slowed as he approached the pier, where Varden waited, standing tall above the crates.

"Tom!" He called as he hurried over. *I was worried.*

"You were waiting for me?" Tomás asked as he approached.

"Yes, when you weren't on the ship...it was concerning. While we are not leaving for a few days, there is quite a bit of animosity toward those like you."

"Yes, I noticed."

Varden wrung his hands together. "When history runs deep, it is hard to shake such conceptions. It is hard to find trust."

"They trusted you quite fast."

"Well, they have had experience with seers. Some of them even worked alongside Kek for a time."

"So, you knew them?"

"Me? No. That was before me—after all, Kek dabbles with immortality."

*And disrupts the very essence of Life and Death,* Tomás thought but did not say aloud. Instead, he replied, "Then some are immortal?"

"Yes, which is why they are familiar with the seers that work alongside Kek."

Tomás furrowed his brow, pondering. "When you mentioned the vision...Yusef mentioned how he wasn't sure if he would see a seer again. Does that have to do with Kek?"

Varden's face hardened, his gaze locking onto the edge of the dock. At first, Tomás thought he was entering another trance, but then he said, "There is no good side in this war between Kek and Ningursu, Tom. You must understand that. Kek has used seers for centuries to further their own power, using us to create their source of power: In Domumus Divitiae."

"What is In Domumus Divitiae? It sounds familiar."

"In Domumus Divitiae, a pool of powerful liquid which grants not only immortality but is used to create so much more. It is part of the reason for this ongoing battle between Kek and Ningursu. My understanding is that the two disagreed on its use...but that may not be the complete story." Varden paced a few steps forward, grazing his hand over a nearby crate. "What I have learned is that any seer who helps enhance In Domumus Divitiae faces a life of torture. I am fortunate that my powers did not adhere to Kek's desires."

Tomás stared up at Varden. Despite his height, he curled in on himself, appearing rather small against the backdrop of the sea. He placed a hand on his friend's arm.

Varden continued without flinching. "There is no good side to this war. It is just two sides, enthralled with power, fighting over stories that have long since disappeared from the earth. We are mere casualties, left to do our duty...while we wait for a hero to arrive."

"Do you mean L'Corona Verde?" asked Tomás.

"I saw her in my vision, but I believe there are others who will fight along her side."

"But we do not know when they will come?"

"No one does. That is the problem with being a seer." Varden's shoulders fell. "We see many things, but there is no timeline to them. L'Corona Verde could arrive tomorrow, next year, in a century, or even in a millennium. We cannot be certain. So, we wait."

Tomás glanced back toward the city of São Caméliosa. The voices hummed, as if singing a distant song for L'Corona Verde, waiting...

For someone to lift the Mist.

For someone to bring the Green.

And for someone to restore what had been stolen from them.

.

# THIRTY-FOUR

For the remaining days in port, Tomás and Varden adhered to their own duties. While Varden returns to the Gardeniros to recant his vision, Tomás retreated to the forests, releasing the dead just as he had back on the Schanifeld. This was his talent, after all; while he could not stop whatever war brewed in the distance, he could at least release souls, save the dead, and continue on with his duties.

Waiting for peace.

Waiting for safety.

Waiting for a constant amid chaos.

So, he released souls and listened to the constant blathering of voices. It was nice, in a way; he hid in the Mist and took in the world, never quite visible to the naked eye. No one watched as he stumbled with his half-blinded sight. Like Ningursu or Aelia, he could operate in the shadows.

But they changed the world while he was just...here.

Ningursu had not selected him as one of the most talented; Cevin was the talented one. What good was it to hear voices if he could not change them or guide them?

Yet, he had survived, hadn't he? Even if his magic was just a fraction of the others, he had survived.

It was with that knowledge he continued to release the dead, returning to the ship each night. Varden would wait for him each night, his thoughts layered with excitement at Tomás's arrival. They would climb aboard the ship to share a meal, and as Tomás drank a cup of tea, Varden often sat there in silence, locked in his own reveries. All of it was enough to bring comfort so Tomás did not feel alone.

It was there, on the pier, that Varden said to him one night, "I spoke to Captain Huo. They intend to leave in two days' time."

"To where?"

"They mentioned going toward Sīchóu Shíyóu. There is business to attend there," Varden gazed out toward the water.

"Oh."

"Yusef and some of the Gardeniros are going to join."

"To see if they can find L'Corona Verde?" Tomás asked.

Varden shrugged. "I think some just want to see the world."

"I see." Tomás wrung his hands together and frowned. In the back of his mind, the voices hummed. "I...do not think I will be going, then."

"Pardon?"

"I have souls to release. It is my duty."

"Oh. I see."

They stood there in silence, attention locked on the water, the waves thrashing to each beat of their collective hearts. Tomás opened his mouth a couple times to speak but found nothing to say. This was his journey as a Mist Keeper.

Varden turned back to Tomás, his red eyes shining with the setting sun, "I shall stay with you."

"Varden—"

"Tomás, you are my friend. I think it is important that we stay together," Varden placed a hand on Tomás's shoulder. "I do care for you—I have since we met years ago."

Tomás shrugged Varden's hand away and glanced at his feet. "I know. I never forgot you...after our first meeting."

"Then let me stay with you."

"I cannot be what you want, though," Tomás whispered.

Varden did not reply.

So Tomás continued, "You must understand...I cannot give up on Cevin."

"I know," Varden said. "I would never ask you to. But I am your friend first—and I hope you'll accept me as a constant companion in your life. Besides...no one should wander this world alone."

"I would feel guilty, leading you along like this."

"There is no reason to feel guilty. I shall walk alongside you as a friend," Varden smiled slightly before saying, "Besides...I'm sick of sailing about the world with no purpose. There's more to *see*."

Tomás continued to stare at Varden. The man's smile did not waver. It was the type of smile that did not fill his face but brought light to his eyes. In every aspect, he wanted Varden to join him.

But then he remembered Cevin, lying there sick in the infirmary.

The idea of wandering with someone else did appeal to him though. At least for a time, as he fell into the proper role.

"Very well," Tomás said.

"I can join you?"

"Yes. I will appreciate the companionship."

"Excellent!" Varden's smile extended.

And even Tomás couldn't help but grin.

# THIRTY-FIVE

As the ship left São Caméliosa, Tomás and Varden ventured down the unkempt path, away from the city and into the forest. With the smoke as a cloak, they did not fear any creatures lurking in the forest; from the smallest dragons to the largest rodents, none noticed the seer and the Mist Keeper leaving behind civilization.

They walked with no destination. While Tomás could use the Mist to expedite his journey, they took each day as their own, two friends traversing the rainforests and beaches, one releasing souls and the other peering into the unknown.

Together, they could ignore the war brewing in the distance. Some days, Tomás forgot about it all together.

It was at this pace that time passed. He and Varden, wandering beside each other, more than friends but less than lovers. Every emotion they shared was with honesty and truth, but any time that Tomás got closer to Varden, the mere memory of Cevin drew him away. If he had been a hero, he might have saved Cevin.

Instead, he wandered, seeking his own form of constant peace.

They happened upon many towns, finding refuge in quiet inns and taverns. It was there, over mugs of ale, he and Varden tossed the cloak of formalities aside, telling stories and harboring truths.

Tomás couldn't be sure how many moons had passed when he finally told Varden of everything that had happened at the Phrontistery—from Teodozia's failure to Ningursu and Aelia's monsters. This left Varden quiet, his red eyes distant, pupils like pinpoints.

"I am sorry I did not tell you until now," Tomás finally admitted.

"No. It is all well and good—I understand your hesitation," Varden glanced at Tomás. "I always knew there was something amiss from Cevin's letters to Edith. I guess even I could not fully see the truth."

Tomás picked at his fingers. "I wish I could have helped them. But...when I saw Teodozia that first time...I was scared. I did not know what else to do. My magic is not made for battles. Neither am I."

"We are unaware what is happening on the Schanifeld. It is a different world there."

"Yes, but it is still there...waiting for us." Tomás had seen it in São Caméliosa, surrounded by smoke, and even now, as they wandered, the evidence remained.

It had always been part of Tomás's life. But after traveling with Varden, releasing souls, and meeting the Gardeniros, it was clear to him.

"Perhaps all we can do is hone our magic and continue practicing our skills." Varden lifted his mug of ale to his lips.

"It is not like our magic is a type that can end wars."

Varden finished his drink and placed it on the table. His response arrived in a calm, even tone. "Right now, that is true. But, have either of us truly tested our limitations?"

Tomás stared at his own mug and frowned. "What more can I do but read and communicate with thoughts? It does not seem conducive to anything else."

"What about manipulate them?"

"Manipulate thoughts?"

"Have you never considered it?"

"Never..." Tomás picked at the rim of the mug. How would he even go about manipulating someone's thoughts? And even if he could, what good would that do in an endless war?

It was better to continue his duty, keep his head down, and let the story play out as intended.

Varden did not bring up expanding their magic again. Instead, they continued their wandering all the same. It was hard to keep track of where they were, continuing their journey north, where the land shifted from humidity to tepid, stiff to muddy, and clear to smoky. The conversation about their magic haunted Tomás, though. Had he stopped himself from exploring further, settling into a rhythm? He had learned to communicate with his magic, but was there more? Even Ningursu had hinted there was more. Tomás hadn't acted at the time...but now, if there was a chance to find Cevin...maybe it was something worth exploring.

He walked with that knowledge for moons, releasing souls as they reached out to him. The smoke grew thicker as they left behind the greenery of the swamp, entering the brittle and dry land of Effluvia. Here, the voices never stopped talking, reaching for Tomás. Even Varden lost himself in the smoke, using it as a guide to the future.

One day, as they entered a small village bordering a canyon, a voice cried out.

*My fault.*

Tomás turned to Varden. "I have one more to release, and then we can find food."

"I shall begin looking while you do what you need," Varden replied.

"I'll meet you back here within the hour."

Tomás waited for Varden to disappear down a nearby road, then turned the opposite way, following the echoing voice.

*My fault.*

*It's all my fault.*

The road turned at the canyon, tracking along it into the distance. The voice continued from the canyon, though, echoing and crying the same words.

*It's all my fault.*

*This is better.*

*My fault.*

Tomás stared into the canyon. There was no way down, but the voice remained, a constant echo in his direction. Inhaling the Mist around him, he extended his hand, letting the voice crawl through him.

*I don't deserve to live.*

*It's my fault.*

"It's not your fault," Tomás said as he continued to reach for the voice. "Come with me."

*This is better. It's my fault.*

"It's not your fault."

*It will always be my fault.*

Tomás gritted his teeth. He didn't know why the voice claimed fault, but this resistance would leave it to suffer.

How long could he stand here, arguing with a voice of the dead?

But he would not walk away from it.

*Everything is my fault.*

"Nothing is your fault. You deserved to live."

*I deserved to die.*

"You deserved to live!" He exclaimed, louder this time. Furrowing his brow, he wrapped his thoughts around the voice, casting his own premonitions like a cloak over it.

*Believe me. No one deserves to end everything early. You deserved to live. It wasn't your fault.*

The voice did not respond to him.

*Please, you deserve peace. Come with me.*

Nothing.

*Please.*

The voice finally responded, as soft as the wind on a breezeless day, *It...was...not my fault.*

Tomás closed his hand, letting the Mist gather around it, another soul finally welcoming closure. The smoke momentarily formed the shape of a person, staring hard at Tomás before dissipating to find their peace.

# THIRTY-SIX

Tomás ate his meat and potatoes in silence that
night. Varden sat beside him, sharing that equal silence. The release that evening had been strange, as
if the soul's entire belief system changed.

He placed the bowl down and turned to Varden.

"Something strange happened tonight."

"Oh?" Varden asked.

"When I was releasing the soul, she was adamant
something was her fault. I do not know what it was, but
to help her cross, I told her it wasn't her fault. She remained fixated on that one statement. That is...until I
extended my own belief into her mind."

"What did you say?"

"It was not profound. Merely that none of this was her
fault."

"And that changed her beliefs?"

"It...manipulated them," Tomás poked one of the potatoes with his wooden spoon.

Varden perked up at that, "Do you think that you really altered her way of thinking?"

"It is not like I could test it again."

"Why not?"

"It would be invasive."

Varden leaned forward, pressing his fingers to his lips, thinking. His brow came together, highlighting the enigmatic color of his eyes. In the dim firelight of the tavern, they glowed red, just like his slicked-back hair.

After a moment, he said, "What if you test on me?"

"That would be inappropriate—I already try not to read your thoughts."

"Oh, you are already aware my deepest ones," Varden winked, and his thoughts continued, *I hope one day you'll return those same feelings.*

Tomás glanced at his hands. "Vardy—I cannot—with Cevin—"

"Yes, yes, let's not talk about that," Varden waved his hand. "And I think it is the only way for you to practice."

"But how?"

"Well...you need to change my opinion on something. We can try something inconsequential...like food."

"But how might I go about doing that? What if your opinions are the same as mine?"

Varden scanned the room. "Here's an idea: I'll give you five foods I hate. You need to work to change my mind on one of them...then the next time we happen upon that food, if I choose it, then it worked. And you know I won't be lying...since you can read my thoughts."

Tomás adjusted the edge of his sleeves, then nodded. "That might work."

"So, the five things I hate are..." Varden counted on his fingers before reciting, "Apples, wild rice, pork, carrots, and tea."

"That is quite a strange list."

"What can I say...I have an odd palette."

Tomás chuckled as he committed the list to memory. He didn't have a clue how to go about changing Varden's opinion, but he would try.

That was all he hoped for, anyway.


With winter beginning its icy embrace, Tomás chose tea as his focus. He spent hours pondering the benefits, taste, and warmth of tea. It was easier than fixating on foods, all of which were not remarkable in the slightest. But tea was more than just a drink. Tea was warmth and memories.

Tea was a smile.

Tea brought joy.

As they traveled, he infiltrated Varden's thoughts with small comments.

*Doesn't a cup of tea sound good right now?*

*I would really like a nice warm cup.*

*No sugar, no milk, just an aromatic herb warming inside of me.*

He kept the thoughts low, like a hum in the back of Varden's mind. If Varden heard them, he did not react, and when they reached the tavern at night, he opted for his usual mug of ale or a glass of wine.

Not tea.

For a while, Tomás thought it was for naught. That one release might have been a fluke, a coincidence, nothing more.

One frigid day, he and Varden entered a small tavern in a mountain town. Varden removed his cloak, then sat at a table, kicking his snow-covered boots off with a sigh.

"It's freezing out there," he remarked. "Maybe we ought to stay here for a few days."

"I agree," Tomás removed his own cloak and folded it onto the chair. "Do you want me to get you an ale?"

"Actually...I've really been wanting tea lately."

Tomás froze. "What?"

"Tea. I want tea."

"But...you hate tea."

"I..." Varden blinked, then smiled, "Tom!"

"You really want a cup of tea? You're not humoring me?"

"No—you did it! You altered my opinions! I really want that cup of tea!" Varden laughed, deep and full. It was a low rumble, a rare occurrence, like an earthquake.

"Well, I suppose I'll get you that cup of tea."

"Please do!"

Tomás smiled, yet as he turned, it faded. Wars rarely met their end over a cup of tea.

But at least it was a start.

# THIRTY-SEVEN

With Varden's permission, Tomás kept practicing, altering his opinions of apples, wild rice, and carrots. It took less time with each food, and by the time Tomás reached carrots, the change in opinion occurred in less than one day.

*You're amazing, Tomás. Really.* Varden's praising thoughts remained constant.

If only Varden knew how much Tomás appreciated him. Varden was his first constant, and with the passing time, Tomás often found his thoughts lingering more on Varden than Cevin.

A slither of hope remained that he might one day reunite with Cevin and his silly smile. But there was still Varden beside him. A confidante. A friend.

And more.

Tomás never considered manipulating Varden's feelings. That was far too invasive.

And he didn't even know if he wanted to change them.

Varden infiltrated his dreams. His laughter, his smile, and his perplexing eyes made a permanent mark on Tomás's sleeping mind. He could not shake them.

But he couldn't bring himself to admit his feelings aloud.

So their friendship remained unscathed as they left behind the mountains and the dead, wandering north without purpose or plan.

And, in honesty, that is what Tomás loved the most: the freedom. No destination. No goal.

Freedom.

Peace.

Constantly.

With winter blossoming into a lifeless spring, he and Varden spent more time camping beneath the stars, telling stories of their pasts and pondering the future.

"Do you think you have released the souls of your parents?" Varden asked one day as they sat around a fire.

"Pardon?" Tomás glanced up from the flames.

"Your parents. It has been many years...so do you think you have released their soul?"

Tomás turned his attention to the stars. "Honestly? I have not given my parents a passing thought in many years."

"You never wonder what became of them?"

"Of course I have, but...they abandoned me."

"Do you not have any memory of them?"

Tomás shook his head. "They're like shadows, hidden by the years of voices that marked my childhood. I am sure it was overwhelming for them...so they had to leave me at La Catedral in El Limra."

"Tom, that should have been their last option. They were your parents." Varden placed a hand on Tomás's arm.

They locked their eyes for a moment, but Tomás turned away just as fast.

He replied, "Whoever they were, it doesn't matter. I became who I am now without them...and I do not think I would have traded a moment."

"Neither would I," Varden agreed.

They shared a smile, then lay back beneath the stars, pretending that nothing could disrupt their peaceful night.

Until the storm clouds rolled in the next morning.

A thunderous clap woke them. Tomás sat up at once, the noise echoing in his ear like a voice. It took his good eye a minute to make sense of their surroundings. The sky glowed yellow, shifting with smoke, like the souls that Tomás had released. With another bang, the thunder sent shivers through Tomás's spine, bringing memories of his time at the Phrontistery back to him.

To his time releasing souls alone.

To his time climbing the stairwell.

To his time staring at a monster hidden by his teacher's own hands.

He stumbled to his feet. Beside him, Varden rose, his bottom lip quivering as the storm clouds thickened.

"This is no rainstorm..." Varden whispered.

"No...it's not..." Tomás stared into the clouds. Voices tore around him, echoing on and off, clawing at his ears. They all poured from a figure, sifting through the smoke. It stood as tall as the trees, with yellow eyes and arms too long for its body. Tomás could not make out its face.

"Why is it here?" Varden asked as he stumbled back a few paces.

"I do not know," Tomás continued to watch as the monster circled them. Which of his classmates had transformed?

"Shouldn't we go? Before it attacks?"

Tomás shook his head. He inhaled once, then reached out his thoughts, *Hello?*

A distorted voice responded, echoing a thousand different voices in a single word. *Mine.*

The monstrous figure moved· closer. Through the smoke, Tomás could make out its yellow glowing eyes and unevenly shaped lips.

The same lips he had kissed a thousand times.

Tomás froze in place.

*Mine.* The monster neared Varden, its fingers elongated.

Varden's entire body stiffened as the creature touched his neck.

"Cevin..." Tomás mouthed.

The creature did not reply. It hunched over Varden, making the giant appear small and frail. Varden fell backward into a nearby tree, frozen in place as the smoke leeched to his body.

Tomás gulped and stepped forward, then with the Mist on his fingers, willed his thoughts forward. *Cevin...this isn't what you want to do. Stop.*

The figure paused.

*Cevin, it's me. It's Tom. Stop.*

The monster turned, its haunting stare piercing into him.

*This isn't you.*

They locked their eyes. For just a second, Tomás swore he saw Cevin's silver eyes soften.

Slowly, Tomás approached the monster, holding his thoughts close. *This isn't you.*

It was enough to keep the monster from attacking Varden, enough for Cevin to see him...at least one last time.

The monster shrank as Tomás approached. Without the guise of smoke and Mist, it appeared rather frail, like a skeleton walking.

He held out his hand. The monster did not move.

"I am sorry I couldn't save you, Cevin," Tomás said. Gently, he placed his hand on the monster's malformed face.

It still did not move.

Tomás ran his finger over its crooked lip. Then, he leaned forward and pressed his lips to the monster's mouth.

*Tom.* Cevin's voice echoed. Distorted, but there.

Tomás stepped back from the creature. He wanted to believe that Cevin was there, reaching for him. But there was nothing he could do. Whatever remained of Cevin was but a shadow, like a puddle left over after a rain shower. He gulped, then projected one final thought. *I set you free.*

The creature blinked.

Then, the wind picked up around them, and the yellow storm thickened. It wrapped around the creature, and then, with a final gasp, it dissipated, leaving behind a trail across the early morning sky.

Tomás kneeled on the ground, his body shaking, breath heaving.

Varden crawled over to his side. "Is it...dead?"

"No. I convinced it to be free..." Tomás croaked.

"What does that mean?"

"It means that Cevin will see the world now...free of whatever burden he carried. At peace...I hope."

"Cevin?" Varden placed a hand on Tomás's shoulder. "Are you alright then, Tom?"

Tomás glanced at Varden and shook his head. Tears bubbled at the bottom of his good eye.

"Come here, Tom," Varden opened his arms.

Tomás accepted the embrace, letting his tears take over as he sobbed into Varden's chest.

# THIRTY-EIGHT

Footsteps eventually pulled Tomás from Varden's arms. Dead leaves crunched beneath them, rushing out of the trees.

A figure emerged from the tree line. "Come on, this way! I saw him right over here—you!"

There, with crazed red curls and armor suited for a knight, stood Edith. Behind her, the ghost from the Phrontistery, with a thick beard and distant eyes, followed.

Varden rose, stepping in front of Tomás. "Hello, Edith."

"Get away from that Reaper, Varden. He's the reason for all our problems," Edith snarled.

"Last I checked, you cut open his face."

"And I would do it again."

"He has done nothing wrong."

"Every time I search for Cevin, *he* is there!"

Tomás rose, shaking, "I was there because I loved him!"

Edith rolled her eyes. "Then where is he now?"

"I set him free."

"What does that mean?"

"It means he helped your brother," Varden added. "Tom is not your enemy, Edith."

"All the Reapers are my enemies," she snarled. "You do not know what they can do."

"Tomás didn't do any of that, though."

"But he has the potential. Fuck, he even got you to run off...without me! You know what those damn Reapers did to me while you two were off fucking about? They tortured me! If it wasn't for Nedo helping me escape, I'd still be their prisoner."

"Edith, our choice to leave was not on me. Captain Huo made the decision."

Edith scoffed. Beside her, the ghost called Nedo swayed, his attention toward the sky.

"You know that I have no say in where the ship goes."

"Even so, you have decided to spend time fucking around with this Reaper. You probably do not even know what is going on back on the Schanifeld."

Tomás perked up slightly. He had avoided all thoughts of war, but now, it was hard to ignore. With Cevin's arrival, it had returned to the forefront of his mind. What happened to the others?

"I have always been neutral in the matters of Life and Death," Varden stated.

"And at what cost, Varden?" Edith asked.

"You tell me."

She cackled. "Kek has since used three different seers to extend their power. After you left, they trained that seer, Yeshua...but he ran off with some girl before Kek enhanced his power. Kek was livid and, rather than training another seer, he found three more. They didn't live, Varden. Kek drained their magic and tossed them aside."

Varden's face paled. "How do you know?"

"Nedo saw it all," she motioned to the ghost.

The ghost bowed his head but did not say a word.

"Kek has gone mad," Edith continued. "They're desperate. The Reapers are rising in power every day. You should see what they have done to the Schanifeld."

"What is happening?" Tomás asked, peeking out from behind Varden, gripping his friend's arm.

Edith chuckled again. "Wouldn't you like to know?"

Varden interjected, "Edith—what is happening on the Schanifeld?"

"Death."

Varden groaned.

She smirked.

"Edith..."

"Monsters are everywhere, Varden. They're eating magic, taking life from flowers, and leaving death in their wake. What more can I say?"

"Monsters like Cevin..." Tomás whispered.

"We got him out before he got too bad...but now you've gone and 'set him free.'" Edith glowered at Tomás.

He glanced away.

"Kek has lost countless members of their Palaver. Honestly, the least we could do is cut open this Reaper's neck to even the playing field a bit." Edith removed a knife from her belt. As she pulled it, the object extended into a full-length sword.

"That won't solve anything," Varden hissed.

"It would make me really happy."

*No. It won't.* Tomás pushed his thoughts forward, letting them wrap around Edith.

"But for now, I'll let it be." She placed her sword back on her belt. It shrank back to the size of a knife. "You two cannot hide from this war any longer, though. If you want to keep on living, I suggest you come with me to Merton."

"Why?" Varden asked.

# THIRTY-NINE

With Edith's sword pointed at them, Tomás and Varden had no other choice but to follow her to the east, where the smoke had grown thick, and the trees no longer bore leaves. Death waited, a stain on the world, as it had waited back in São Caméliosa.

Tomás stayed close to Varden. At night, they slept side-by-side, taking shifts to watch Edith and Nedo. While the ghost showed no signs of malice, rarely speaking, it was hard to trust him. His thoughts remained jumbled, hopping between past and present, guided by an ancient language.

Edith, on the other hand, wore her thoughts on her sleeve.

"You know, Reaper, you'd look better if you let me cut out that other eye," she chided by the fire one night.

Another day, she hammered into him, "If you loved my brother so much, why not join him? Die. Give up this horrible life."

And, "I think you caused Cevin to fail. He was too focused on his frail little Tom that he didn't put energy into success."

Varden eventually stepped in, "Edith...enough! None of this is Tomás's fault."

She smirked.

Tomás did not humor her taunts, his head down as he watched the fire wane to embers. She might have been right, of course; if Cevin had spent more time focusing on his duty as a Mist Keeper, he might have met success with a smile.

Varden placed a hand on Tomás's arm as Edith waltzed off into the woods. "Do not hold guilt over your success, Tom. You are fantastic."

Tomás grimaced and poked at the fire with a nearby stick.

"She is but trying to bother you and cast doubt. Do not let her."

"I know," Tomás replied, "but it does not stop my heart from aching."

To his surprise, Nedo spoke from the other side of the fire, his voice deep and unpracticed, "He wanted nothing more than you to succeed. Do not be guilt's prisoner."

Tomás stared at the ghost.

But the conversation ended with that statement.

He wore that statement close, holding it like a new-born baby as they continued wandering, from moon-to-moon, through the brittle forest. A distant memory of Cevin's voice echoed in his head; he imagined Cevin saying exactly what Nedo insinuated.

And despite Edith's rude remarks, he began to chisel away at the guilt congesting his heart so that at night, he might rest his head on Varden's shoulder and sleep with nightmares of a life once lived.

With the heavy weight of summer arriving, the trees grew few and far between while white flowers bloomed between their roots. The Schanifeld arrived like a trickling rain. As the trees parted, the flowers returned, scattering for miles across the rolling plains.

Yet here, the flowers did not extend like snow. Rather, splotches of black, wilting petals cut the Schanifeld like a grid. Smoke rose from their stems, life leeched from their bodies. As Tomás walked forward, the dead flowers tacked to his body, a group of subjects begging for Death's attention and care.

From their spot on the hill, a city emerged into their view, perched over a red sea.

"Merton...the Capital of Magic," Varden said.

Tomás reached for his friend's wrist.

"Don't be afraid, Tom."

"I have only heard the stories that Ningursu and Aelia preached."

"I am sure they are wrong."

"Oh, they are wrong. Don't worry," Edith hissed. "But you should be scared. Doubt anyone will be happy to see a Reaper walking amongst them."

"Perhaps I shouldn't go," Tomás said.

"Oh no, you're coming. Now. Follow me," Edith removed her blade again.

"There's no reason for threats, Edith. We're following," Varden grumbled.

She poked Tomás's back with her sword, "But is he?"

"Edith, stop," Nedo said, a few paces back from them. "Let us continue."

They descended the hill. Tomás remained quiet, staying close to Varden's side, eyes locked on the city in the distance. The hum of voices crawled up his neck.

"So, what is the plan here, Edith?" Varden asked. "I am neutral in these affairs, you know."

"Kek does not support neutrality anymore. They have already brought Captain Huo and their crew back to Merton. To be neutral is to be on the opposing side," Edith stopped a few paces forward, turning around to grin at

Tomás. "I am sure Kek will want to do some investigations on our little Reaper friend here."

"Edith, this is not productive," Nedo said again.

She cackled but said no more.

As they crossed a bridge over the canal leading into the city, Tomás took hold of Varden's hand. He expected Merton to be something oozing with grandeur, but instead, it was like any other city on the Schanifeld. With its wooden framed buildings, shingled roofs, and cobblestone walkways, it transported Tomás back to the village beneath the Phrontistery.

The only thing that set them apart was the intricate fountains, bubbling in each plaza with silver.

Tomás slowed as they rounded the first one. In the dim light, the liquid did not look any different from water. But, as he stared at it, he recalled Aelia's private study, where she examined his magic. There, a basin of silver liquid provided her insight.

A silver liquid that looked just the same as what bubbled in the fountain.

Varden joined Tomás's side, "In Domumus Divitiae. Kek's creation."

"The one that grants immortality?" Tomás asked.

"And more. It is Kek's very essence of power and magic. They built these fountains so all with magic might access it."

"And become immortal?"

"Immortal and stronger. The uses for In Domumus Divitiae are unlimited."

"No wonder Ningursu is scared...that threatens the balance if anyone can be immortal."

Edith laughed. "Kek only created this to fend off Ningursu's growing power."

Varden shook his head.

Behind them, Nedo whispered, "Neither side is right in their decisions. Too much power corrupts even the wisest minds."

Every time the ghost spoke, it sent shivers through Tomás's body. Nedo had knowledge that extended beyond even Varden's understanding. How? Tomás could not quite make sense of the odd feeling in his chest. There was something familiar about him, but what? He wasn't sure.

They continued through the quiet paths of the city. Tomás ignored the voices whispering to him, thumping on the side of his head like a persistent headache. When was the last time the souls of this city found their peace? Had they been locked away, succumbing to their own nightmares for centuries?

He slowed as they came to the water. The red waves of the sea crawled to shore, painting the pristine white sand. At the pier, boats bobbed on the surface, including Captain Huo's ship.

"We're all here then," Varden remarked.

Tomás did not reply, keeping his attention locked in the distance.

Past the water.

Toward the horizon.

Where yellow storm clouds gathered.

Waiting to attack.

# FORTY

Tom...do you see that?" Varden asked, following Tomás's gaze toward the horizon.

"Yes," Tomás acknowledged. In the distance, voices gathered, crawling over each other, with one destination in mind.

*It tastes close.*

The voices overlapped each other. If Tomás focused hard enough, he swore he heard his peers from the Phrontistery chattering away. All uniform.

One group.

Approaching.

"We need to stop it..." Tomás whispered. "It's coming here."

"How do we go about doing that?"

Tomás met Varden's eyes, "I'll go...try to convince it to turn around."

"I am coming too, then."

"No!" Tomás grabbed Varden's arm. "It will affect you far more than me. Warn everyone here to hide—if magic is as prevalent as you say, then everyone is at risk."

Varden nodded, then stole a quick glance in Edith's direction. She had walked a few paces forward, dragging her fingers along a nearby iron fence. Nedo floated behind her, his gaze toward the horizon as well.

"I'll distract Edith. Go...and be safe," Varden said.

Tomás placed a hand on Varden's shoulder. Standing on his tiptoes, he directed Varden's gaze toward him and planted a quick kiss on his lips.

"Tom..." Varden mouthed.

"I will see you soon," Tomás stepped back from Varden. After a brief smile, he let the Mist wrap around him and transport him from the city.

He stumbled onto the Schanifeld. It had been many years since he had used the Mist as a method of transport, and the act of solidifying left him rocking on his feet. He gripped a small tree to maintain his balance, then exhaled. There he stood, amongst the white flowers, on a hill overlooking the valley. In the west, the outline of

Merton against the red sea peaked through the gathering smoke.

Tomás turned to the storm. Figures pulsed in and out, a singular entity operating with multiple bodies. This was everything that Ningursu had worked on, wasn't it? He wanted to build an army. Perhaps, at first, it was an army of Mist Keepers. But now he had these nameless monsters, moving like a hurricane, sniffing out anything that dared threaten the balance.

In all honesty, Tomás hadn't a clue who was right or wrong. Was Kek too powerful, giving Life a chance to exist for eternity? Or was Ningursu disrupting the way of magic and leaving the world brittle and brown?

Tomás knew, though, that fighting like this would not cause anything more than blood.

He brought his hands together, then closed his eyes. The words he selected would be key. This was not Cevin, not Varden; these were his peers, left to rot, while he was free.

*You will not find peace here.*

The wind bellowed.

*This is not your salvation.*

A gust caught his cloak, sending his hood over his ears.

*Scatter.*

*Scatter.*

*Scatter!*

His eyes flew open, and the final thought exited his lips, booming, "Now!"

The storm hung there, a single streak of lightning illuminating the countless shadows within it.

"Go...I set you free," Tomás murmured.

The voices spiraled around him in response.

*Free...*

*This way!*

*That way!*

*North!*

*West!*

*Free...*

   *Free...*

      *Free.*

With a thunderous clap that knocked Tomás off his feet, the storm caved in on itself.

Tomás's final thought echoed as the monsters dispersed, leaving behind a yellow hue and a gentle dance of fog. *Say hello to Cevin for me.*

# FORTY-ONE

Tomás lay in the bed of wilted flowers, heaving. While he wouldn't go as far as to say he defeated the monsters, he did disperse them.

For now, they had another quest.

Scatter.

Be free.

Find Cevin.

He hoped that, until he and Varden discovered how to disrupt the monster in its entirety, that would be enough.

He laughed to himself. Just a mere thought derailed a monster! What else could it do?

It was frightening but powerful. What would all those children at La Catedral think now? What about Ningursu? Or Aelia?

He had potential.

He had reached it.

Tomás pulled himself off the ground and squinted into the fading yellow smoke. From his hilltop, the valley extended beyond him, checkered with white flowers and black smudges. A figure raced across the Schanifeld on horseback, heading away from Merton, their white cloak gusting around them.

*This is my chance.* Their voice carried from across the Schanifeld, resting right in the center of Tomás's mind.

Behind the figure, others rode on horseback, a battle cry solidifying in their minds. They all traveled fast, weaving in and out of the smoke toward where the flowers had turned black, and the smoke rose like ink, dripping in rage.

*And so, the war continues,* he thought to himself, taking a step back from the edge of the hill. What might he do to end it? At least, with the monsters, he guided them to a moment of peace.

He started his descent from the hill, away from the ever-growing rumble of war. His head pounded from the barrage of thoughts, and as he walked, it was as though he had fallen back into the echoes of his past, locked in La Catedral, with the voices of his only friend. He stroked the edge of his cloak.

Varden waited for him in Merton, and from there, they'd continue their journey.

Together.

Closer than ever.

He held onto that excitement as he trudged through the dying flowers. Any energy he had to use the Mist had vanished with the monsters.

With his thoughts wandering, he did not hear any other voices approach.

Until a shrill statement rang in his ears, "You!"

He stopped. The hair on his arms rose.

"Tomás! Look at me. Now."

He turned. Aelia stood there, her usually kempt hair hanging in long, matted strands. Her dark eyes narrowed.

"Where have you been? You vanished after that loon Edith attacked."

"I had to heal," Tomás whispered.

"For twenty-seven years?"

"Has it really been that long?" Tomás said. He hadn't kept track of time. With Varden's immortality and his stasis in death, age was nothing more but an inconsequential number.

Aelia continued to glower at him. "You betrayed us. We needed you."

"I was never one for war."

"We transformed you—you owed us your loyalty."

Tomás shook his head, "No. If you were responsible for my transformation, then everyone would have succeeded. You turned them into monsters instead of giving them peace."

"You were a child, rotting away to the voices when we found you."

"Yes, and I owe you my thanks...but the ones who helped me grow were my friends. Cevin, Varden...they gave me what I needed."

"Well, you must come with me now," Aelia grabbed Tomás's arm.

He pulled away from her. "No. I have done fine without you or Ningursu. I am not part of your war."

"We will need your help in finding our creations. Did you not see that they dispersed?"

"Oh, I know. I instructed them to leave."

Aelia's face twisted, and she shouted, "Why would you do that!?"

"They were suffering!"

"Now they will terrorize the world—we contained them, using them as a targeted attack. You have made the most unwise decision, Tomás!"

Tomás glanced at the sky, still tinged yellow. "You are the one that created them. I merely stopped them from upending the balance."

"What are you implying?"

"We should not be acting as Gods in this balance of Life and Death. I have traveled for years now, releasing souls and seeing how the world has changed. We should be guides, not gods."

Aelia grabbed Tomás's wrist, digging her fingernails into his skin. "To not acknowledge our stance allows the opposition to win. Neutrality means you support them."

"I do not support them. They have misused their powers."

"If others take the same opinion, then there will never be balance in this world. I cannot let you preach such nonsense." She dug her fingernails deeper. "I can dismantle you, Tomás. I feel your heartbeat; I know how the Mist runs through you. Be wise with what you say next."

Tomás stared hard at Aelia. His thoughts echoed, *You will let go of me.*

Aelia smirked. "And do not try your magic on me. I have been here for many moons longer than you, child. My magic surpasses yours."

Tomás changed the direction of his thoughts, still with his eyes locked on Aelia. *To reach neutrality is to grant the world a chance to breathe. This needs to end. You will let go of me.*

Aelia's face flickered, yet she did not rescind.

*We cannot find balance in war. We need to breathe.*

She exhaled, her gaze falling to the Schanifeld behind Tomás. Her grip did not lighten.

*Breathe.*

Her next breath did not come with ease but with an exasperated gasp.

Tomás followed her gaze across the Schanifeld.

The figure cloaked in white road on horseback through the flowers, red staining their outfit. Beside them, another figure followed.

He recognized the second figure as Edith in an instant. She shook her loose orange curls back, a sword outstretched, pointing towards Merton in the distance.

Aelia's scream came before Tomás noticed what sat on Edith's sword.

His mouth dropped.

There, perched like a prize, was Ningursu's head...dripping with blood.

# FORTY-TWO

Aelia screeched, dropping Tomás's arm and flying through the Mist toward the entourage in the distance. Tomás did not take time to think, racing after her into the fray. Her screams carried, crazed and manic, while the smoke twisted around her like a tornado.

The wind knocked the horses off their feet as Aelia landed. Tomás halted a few feet behind her, grabbing a nearby tree for support against the bellowing wind.

As the horses whinnied, Edith toppled to the ground, her sword flew, and right at Tomás's feet, landed Ningursu's decapitated head.

Ningursu's eyes shifted. He smirked.

"Senhor?" Tomás whispered.

He closed his eyes, his lips still curved.

"YOU!" Aelia shrieked as she approached the white cloaked figure on the ground. "HOW DARE YOU!"

The white cloaked figure rose and lowered their hood. They spoke with a hint of pride. "Hello, Aelia. It has been some time."

"Oh, do not humor me, Kek."

The figure smiled. With their narrow jaw, curled hair, and dark eyes, there was nothing that remarkable about them.

Then again, was there anything that remarkable about Ningursu?

Tomás lifted Ningursu's head from the ground. Blood dripped from the incision at the head's neck, dripping down Tomás's tunic and down the edges of his cloak.

*Welcome back, Tomás.* Ningursu's voice echoed.

He swallowed.

"As far as I can tell, I won this war. It would be best for you to leave, Aelia...before I do the same to you," Kek said.

"I am a greater alchemist than you will ever be," Aelia hissed.

*Petty bickering. They used to do this all the time.* Ningursu's voice said.

"What does that matter? Ningursu is gone," Kek chuckled. Beside them, Edith and the others joined.

"But he left me with the means to continue his legacy."

Tomás stepped back. *This will never end. It needs to stop. We need peace.*

Kek removed their sword from their hilt and held it out to Aelia's throat. "It would be easy to end that."

The smoke rose at Aelia's feet.

*The world needs to breathe. We need peace.*

"Do not be so certain," Aelia hissed.

*Neither side will win.*

In Tomás's hands, Ningursu's jaw tensed. The head breathed out, a plume of black on its lips.

Then, in a haunting whisper, it spoke.

"This will not end."

Kek and Aelia both froze.

Ningursu continued, his voice hoarse, "We must propose a truce...for the survival of Life and Death."

"Sire!?" Aelia exclaimed.

*A truce is the only way to ensure survival.* Tomás chose each of his thoughts with care.

"We cannot fight like this for all eternity. We will all end up dismembered," Ningursu said.

"Are you only saying that because you lost?" Edith hissed from behind Kek.

"My magic is still sound."

*Even a dismembered corpse does not end a war.* Tomás kept his face calm as he ran through his thoughts.

Kek spoke this time, "If Ningursu is still here, and his magic is still functioning, it means even slicing and dicing our opponents cannot end a war. I am inclined to agree—we must reach a truce, for the sake of Life and Death."

Edith gawked. Aelia's face darkened as she glanced briefly at Tomás.

Tomás did not flinch.

"Then what shall we do now?" Kek asked.

"We will need a neutral source to doctor our treaty. One person that we can trust, on both sides of the aisle," Ningursu's eye met Tomás's face. "I shall select Tomás to represent Aelia and me."

Kek nodded, "I shall seek out someone on my side."

Tomás interjected, "Varden would be a wise choice if I may provide my opinion."

"Very well. Draft your terms—we shall draft ours. Let this finally meet a peaceful end."

Kek grabbed the reins of their horse, then with a swift mount, rode off toward Merton. Edith snarled at Tomás, then followed, with their other allies close behind them.

Aelia snatched Ningursu's head from Tomás. Like a newborn child, she cradled it close, murmuring in an indistinct tongue.

Tomás watched, his heart pounding in his ears. Peace was here; they didn't need a Forest Queen or a bloody battle.

Only one thought, enough to change the direction of fate.

Molded.

Manipulated.

Pacified.

For now.

.

# FORTY-THREE

The terms of the truce took weeks to finalize. Tomás and Varden each took their role in the discussions with silent pride, collecting the terms, then in their shared room at night, scouring through each draft by candlelight. They fell asleep often next to each other, head on shoulders, hands grazing.

They used peace as a guise for intimacy.

And used the treaty as a disguise for communication.

The final doctrine extended the length of a scroll inscribed in Varden's articulate handwriting. Kek and Ningursu had agreed upon the terms in separate conversations.

Only the signatures remained.

Tomás walked close to Varden as they reached the edge of the Schanifeld, just outside of Merton. There,

Aelia waited, with Nedo standing beside her. Nedo held Ningursu in his hands, silent. Side-by-side, their resemblance was uncanny. Even with Ningursu's sinking skin and fraying hair, already stained by his decapitation, it was hard to shake the similarities.

Varden's voice echoed, *I didn't realize they were brothers.*

*They're brothers?* Tomás asked.

*It's obvious now—it is why Ningursu requested Nedo.*

Tomás eyed Ningursu and Nedo. Why hadn't he noticed?

Not that it mattered now.

They stood there in silence as Kek approached on horseback from Merton alone. They dismounted and joined Varden's side.

No one spoke as Varden opened the scroll. The words coated the parchment, each person reading over the words in silence.

*As promised by Life and Death, on the plains of white and black, the One War—as it shall be named—has come to an end on the seventh moon of the six-hundredth-and-seventy-third year.*

*With the support of peacekeepers, Tomás the Custocaligo and Varden the Seer of Delilah, this treaty has been established.*

The terms below have been agreed upon by Tehuti Thema Tarek Kamilah Kafele Kek and Ningursu of Effluvia. Any violation nullifies this truce.

(I)     In Domumus Divitiae shall be split. One barrel to the Council of Custocaligo and one barrel to the Palaver of Immortals. The remainder shall be transported by a neutral party, with its location known only to a select few.

(II)    Creatures assembled from those who failed life at the Phrontistery shall be destroyed within the next one hundred years. No others shall be created from the failures of the Phrontistery.

(III)   Immortality shall be limited to one individual every fifty years.

(IV)    No Seer shall meet their end to support the progression of In Domumus Divitiae.

(V)     The Phrontistery shall be discontinued. Disciples shall be taught on an individual basis.

(VI)    An appointee will be selected as the steed for Ningursu of Effluvia after an unfortunate injury.

(VII)   Merton will remain as a haven for those with magic, not to be touched by the Council of Custocaligo.

(VIII)  Custocaligo will not interfere with the affairs of the living. When possible, Custocaligo will remain part of the Mist, unseen to the natural living eyes. All Custocaligo must remain loyal to their council.

(IX)  Both sides will discontinue their roles in religious expansion across the world. Immortality shall be a secret to those not integrated. The Custocaligo shall be legends to those unfamiliar.

(X)  No known relationships may proceed between those on opposing sides of Life and Death. Custocaligo must remain in the Mist, while all others shall only walk the line of the living. Only the peacekeepers, as so dictated by this treaty, shall communicate in the most formal of matters.

The document extended for multiple pages, reciting details and clauses for each term. Varden flipped through each one, letting Ningursu and Kek read them and ask any final questions.

But there were no questions.

No complaints.

Even if Tomás wanted to protest any of the terms, he could not. As he and Varden wrote the words, his stomach dropped, and skin crawled. But this was for the best.

After all, this was for peace.

For prosperity.

For pacification.

Even if it meant losing his constant.

"Is the treaty appropriate?" Varden asked at last.

No one objected.

Tomás removed a vial of ink and a quill from his cloak. Kek was the first to step forward, taking the quill and scribbling their full name across the document. Next, Nedo carried Ningursu over to the inkwell. He helped his brother dunk his nose into the ink, then press it to the page.

Varden went next. He met Tomás's eyes as he removed the quill. His eyes shook, holding back tears.

*We will continue, Varden,* Tomás thought.

Varden's lips twitched, and then he signed the document.

This left only Tomás.

He took the quill from Varden and, with a final nod, etched his name across the treaty, solidifying peace for the future.

# FORTY-FOUR

Tomás sat at the edge of the pier with Varden, watching as Captain Huo's crew loaded barrels of In Domumus Divitiae onto their ship. He had fallen into silence after signing the treaty. It sat in the pocket of his cloak now, a permanent fixture that marked the new path of his life.

Varden placed his hand over Tomás's hand. They did not need to speak. It was what they had to do; soon, Varden would board the ship, the neutral face of Kek's brigade, and Tomás would join Ningursu and Aelia in finding a new home for their little council. Two worlds, separated by a thin piece of paper.

"Remember, Tomás, we are not without means to communicate," Varden whispered. "You and I are the peacekeepers. It is imperative that we speak."

"In a formal relationship," Tomás replied.

"Yes."

Tomás sighed. "It is hard to think, after all these years together, that we cannot be friends. It is paramount for peace...but..." he shook his head, swallowing. Varden was his constant. He had been his constant when he sailed to the Phrontistery the first time and years later as they transversed the world. It took until Cevin was free for Tomás to see it.

Now, he was losing his constant again.

Varden pulled at the edge of Tomás's cloak. "You still have this."

"It is a memory."

"But it is always there."

Tomás turned back to the ship, refocusing the conversation, "Where do you intend to take In Domumus Divitiae?"

"I am not sure yet. South, probably. The captain has a few ideas."

"I see. It is best that I do not know."

"I would prefer not knowing as well. I may go into hibernation until it is off the ship."

Tomás scoffed.

"Or perhaps I will just stare at the sea, thinking of you," Varden lifted Tomás's chin to face him. "Although I am always thinking of you."

"Constantly," Tomás whispered.

"Constantly."

Tomás swallowed his tears and nodded.

Varden continued, "I will constantly think about how amazing you are, Tomás. You brought peace to Life and Death. Not a mythical Forest Queen. You. Without you...well, we would still be fighting."

Tomás did not reply.

Varden ran a finger down Tomás's face, tracing the scar on his cheek. "I promise you, Tomás, this is but a moment in our lives. We will be together again."

"Is that you trying to make me feel better...or is it truth?"

"Both," Varden smiled.

Tomás stood on his tiptoes and kissed Varden. He savored it, recanting every emotion and feeling as it lingered.

The bell from the ship chimed up the dock. Varden held Tomás, squeezing his hands tight, before releasing him.

"Goodbye, Tomás," Varden said, choking on his tears.

"Until we meet again," Tomás croaked.

They shared one last embrace before Varden hurried up the dock toward the ship.

Tomás watched as he vanished aboard, then turned away from the water and toward the Schanifeld. He pulled his hood over his head. It was time. He had to return to Ningursu and Aelia and take his place as a member of their little council.

But for a moment, he lavished in the silence of the Schanifeld.

It was peaceful. Wonderful.

But empty.

The world had fallen into a slumber.

And the voices had sunk into a distant hum.

Even the Mist danced without disarray.

This was how war ended.

Pacified only by a broken heart.

# WILL THE PEACE TREATY LAST?

*You can find out in*
## THE LIFE & DEATH CYCLE

# THE STORY COLLECTOR'S ALMANAC

## Also by E.S. Barrison...

**Tales from the Effluvium**
*Speak Easy*
*These Sanguine Tides*

**The Unsought Fairytale Collection**

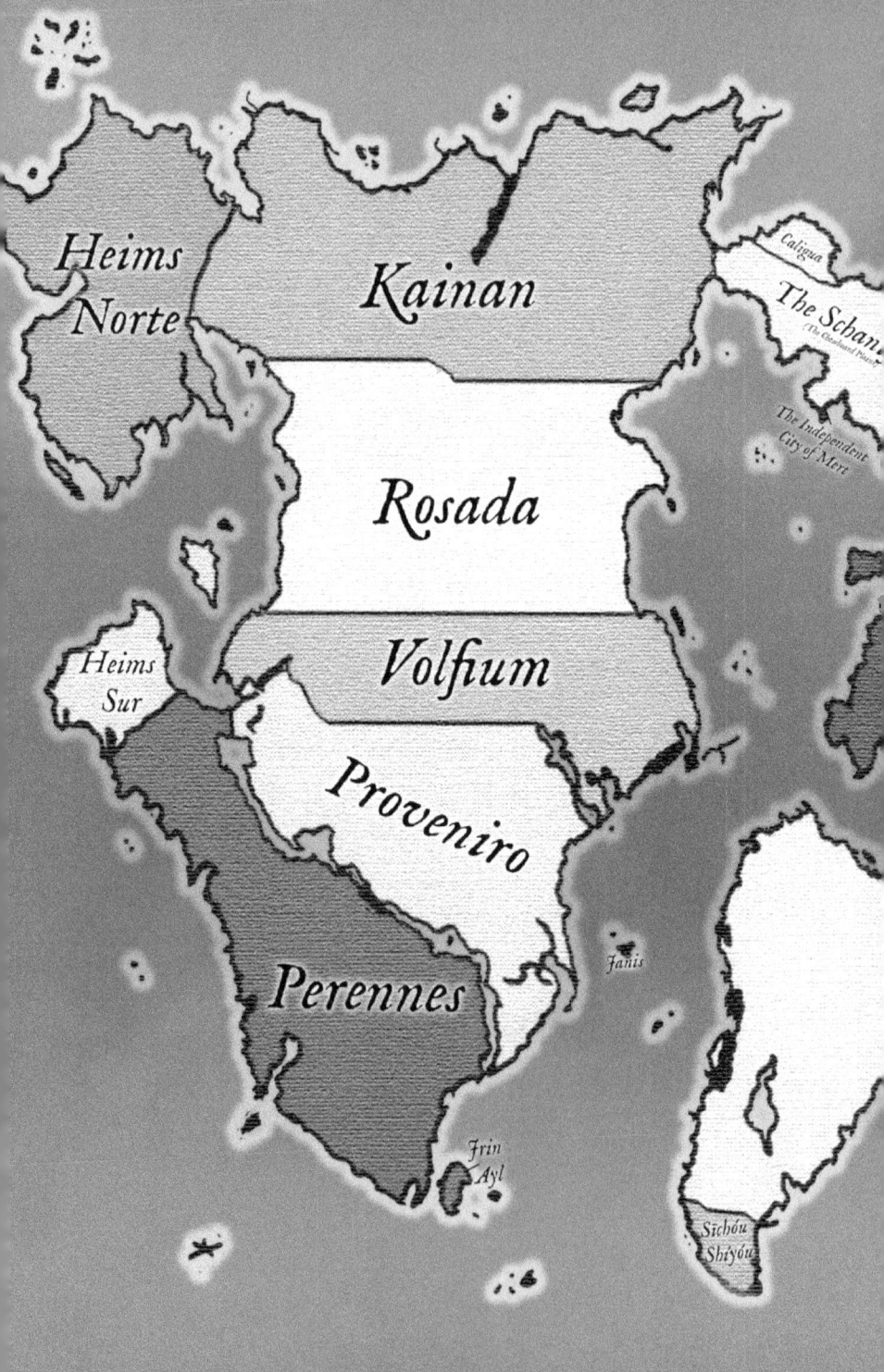

Map of the world at the start of *The Mist Keeper's Apprentice*.

# Author's Note

Thank you so much for taking the time to read *Pacifying the Mist*.

If you enjoyed this book, I would appreciate it if you could:

**Review this book.** Reviews are a great help to an author. If you enjoyed this book, please consider leaving a review online.

**Tell Others.** When you share this book with others on social media, you're allowing others to discover this story. Word-of-mouth is one of the best sources of marketing for an author.

**Connect with me.** If you want to find out about my upcoming releases, stop by my website at www.esbarrison-author.com or connect with me on social media.

Thank you!

E.S. Barrison

# Acknowledgments

To all the following, my thanks, for your support throughout this process:

As always, to Moira, my cover artist – I know these covers aren't easy, but they're always amazing.

To Charlie, my editor, for making this into the story that I wanted to tell.

To Matthew, because you'll read this and gripe about it, but I know you secretly love these stories.

And finally, to my readers, I hope this helps you see the need for quiet heroes.

Without all your support, this story might have never been told.

# About the Author

E.S. Barrison has been writing and creating stories for as long as she can remember. After graduating from the University of Florida, she has spent the past few years wrangling her experiences to compose unique worlds with diverse characters. Currently, E.S. lives in Orlando, Florida with her family.

www.ingramcontent.com/pod-product-compliance
Lightning Source LLC
Chambersburg PA
CBHW071555110726
47908CB00007B/2113